WINSOME WINNIE
AND OTHER NEW
NONSENSE NOVELS

WINSOME WINNIE
AND OTHER NEW NONSENSE NOVELS
BY STEPHEN LEACOCK

LONDON: JOHN LANE, THE BODLEY HEAD
NEW YORK: JOHN LANE COMPANY MCMXXI

Printed in Great Britain by R. Clay & Sons, Ltd., London and Bungay

CONTENTS

		PAGE
I.	*WINSOME WINNIE; OR, TRIAL AND TEMPTATION*	7

CHAP.

I.	THROWN ON THE WORLD . . .	9
II.	A RENCOUNTER	14
III.	FRIENDS IN DISTRESS	18
IV.	A GAMBLING PARTY IN ST. JAMES'S CLOSE	24
V.	THE ABDUCTION	28
VI.	THE UNKNOWN	33
VII.	THE PROPOSAL	36
VIII.	WEDDED AT LAST	42

II.	*JOHN AND I; OR, HOW I NEARLY LOST MY HUSBAND*	43
III.	*THE SPLIT IN THE CABINET; OR, THE FATE OF ENGLAND* . .	65
IV.	*WHO DO YOU THINK DID IT? OR, THE MIXED-UP MURDER MYSTERY*	95

I.	HE DINED WITH ME LAST NIGHT .	97
II.	I MUST SAVE HER LIFE . . .	100
III.	I MUST BUY A BOOK ON BILLIARDS .	108

Contents

CHAP.		PAGE
IV.	THAT IS NOT BILLIARD CHALK	112
V.	HAS ANYBODY HERE SEEN KELLY?	113
VI.	SHOW ME THE MAN WHO WORE THOSE BOOTS	119
VII.	OH, MR. KENT, SAVE ME!	123
VIII.	YOU ARE PETER KELLY	127
IX.	LET ME TELL YOU THE STORY OF MY LIFE	132
X.	SO DO I	139
V.	BROKEN BARRIERS; OR, RED LOVE ON A BLUE ISLAND	143
VI.	THE KIDNAPPED PLUMBER: A TALE OF THE NEW TIME	177
VII.	THE BLUE AND THE GREY: A PRE-WAR WAR STORY	205
VIII.	BUGGAM GRANGE: A GOOD OLD GHOST STORY	225

I

WINSOME WINNIE

OR, TRIAL AND TEMPTATION

(Narrated after the best models of 1875)

CHAPTER I

THROWN ON THE WORLD

"MISS WINNIFRED," said the Old Lawyer, looking keenly over and through his shaggy eyebrows at the fair young creature seated before him, "you are this morning twenty-one."

Winnifred Clair raised her deep mourning veil, lowered her eyes and folded her hands.

"This morning," continued Mr. Bonehead, "my guardianship is at an end."

There was a tone of something like emotion in the voice of the stern old lawyer, while for a moment his eye glistened with something like a tear which he hastened to remove with

9

something like a handkerchief. "I have therefore sent for you," he went on, "to render you an account of my trust."

He heaved a sigh at her, and then, reaching out his hand, he pulled the woollen bell-rope up and down several times.

An aged clerk appeared.

"Did the bell ring?" he asked.

"I think it did," said the Lawyer. "Be good enough, Atkinson, to fetch me the papers of the estate of the late Major Clair defunct."

"I have them here," said the clerk, and he laid upon the table a bundle of faded blue papers, and withdrew.

"Miss Winnifred," resumed the Old Lawyer, "I will now proceed to give you an account of the disposition that has been made of your property. This first document refers to the sum of two thousand pounds left to you by your great uncle. It is lost."

Winnifred bowed.

"Pray give me your best attention and I will endeavour to explain to you how I lost it."

"Oh, sir," cried Winnifred, "I am only a

poor girl unskilled in the ways of the world, and knowing nothing but music and French ; I fear that the details of business are beyond my grasp. But if it is lost, I gather that it is gone."

"It is," said Mr. Bonehead. "I lost it in a marginal option in an undeveloped oil company. I suppose that means nothing to you."

"Alas," sighed Winnifred, "nothing."

"Very good," resumed the Lawyer. "Here next we have a statement in regard to the thousand pounds left you under the will of your maternal grandmother. I lost it at Monte Carlo. But I need not fatigue you with the details."

"Pray spare them," cried the girl.

"This final item relates to the sum of fifteen hundred pounds placed in trust for you by your uncle. I lost it on a horse race. That horse," added the Old Lawyer with rising excitement, "ought to have won. He was coming down the stretch like blue—but there, there, my dear, you must forgive me if the recollection of it still stirs me to anger. Suffice it to say the horse fell. I have kept for your inspection the score card of the race, and the betting tickets. You will find everything in order."

"Sir," said Winnifred, as Mr. Bonehead proceeded to fold up his papers, "I am but a poor inadequate girl, a mere child in business, but tell me, I pray, what is left to me of the money that you have managed?"

"Nothing," said the Lawyer. "Everything is gone. And I regret to say, Miss Clair, that it is my painful duty to convey to you a further disclosure of a distressing nature. It concerns your birth."

"Just Heaven!" cried Winnifred, with a woman's quick intuition. "Does it concern my father?"

"It does, Miss Clair. Your father was not your father."

"Oh, sir," exclaimed Winnifred. "My poor mother! How she must have suffered!"

"Your mother was not your mother," said the Old Lawyer gravely. "Nay, nay, do not question me. There is a dark secret about your birth."

"Alas," said Winnifred, wringing her hands, "I am, then, alone in the world and penniless."

"You are," said Mr. Bonehead, deeply moved. "You are, unfortunately, thrown upon the world. But, if you ever find yourself in a position where you need help and advice, do not scruple to come to me. Especially," he added, "for advice. And meantime let me ask you in what way do you propose to earn your livelihood?"

"I have my needle," said Winnifred.

"Let me see it," said the Lawyer.

Winnifred showed it to him.

"I fear," said Mr. Bonehead, shaking his head, "you will not do much with that."

Then he rang the bell again.

"Atkinson," he said, "take Miss Clair out and throw her on the world."

CHAPTER II

A RENCOUNTER

As Winnifred Clair passed down the stairway leading from the Lawyer's office, a figure appeared before her in the corridor, blocking the way. It was that of a tall, aristocratic-looking man, whose features wore that peculiarly saturnine appearance seen only in the English nobility. The face, while entirely gentlemanly in its general aspect, was stamped with all the worst passions of mankind.

Had the innocent girl but known it, the face was that of Lord Wynchgate, one of the most contemptible of the greater nobility of Britain, and the figure was his too.

" Ha ! " exclaimed the dissolute Aristocrat, " whom have we here ? Stay, pretty one, and let me see the fair countenance that I divine behind your veil."

" Sir," said Winnifred, drawing herself up proudly, " let me pass, I pray."

" Not so," cried Wynchgate, reaching out and

14

seizing his intended victim by the wrist, " not till I have at least seen the colour of those eyes and imprinted a kiss upon those fair lips."

With a brutal laugh, he drew the struggling girl towards him.

In another moment the aristocratic villain would have succeeded in lifting the veil of the unhappy girl, when suddenly a ringing voice cried, " Hold ! stop ! desist ! begone ! lay to ! cut it out ! "

With these words a tall, athletic young man, attracted doubtless by the girl's cries, leapt into the corridor from the street without. His figure was that, more or less, of a Greek god, while his face, although at the moment inflamed with anger, was of an entirely moral and permissible configuration.

" Save me ! save me ! " cried Winnifred.

" I will," cried the Stranger, rushing towards Lord Wynchgate with uplifted cane.

But the cowardly Aristocrat did not await the onslaught of the unknown.

" You shall yet be mine ! " he hissed in Winnifred's ear, and, releasing his grasp, he rushed with a bound past the rescuer into the street.

"Oh, sir," said Winnifred, clasping her hands and falling on her knees in gratitude. "I am only a poor inadequate girl, but if the prayers of one who can offer naught but her prayers to her benefactor can avail to the advantage of one who appears to have every conceivable advantage already, let him know that they are his."

"Nay," said the stranger, as he aided the blushing girl to rise, "kneel not to me, I beseech. If I have done aught to deserve the gratitude of one who, whoever she is, will remain for ever present as a bright memory in the breast of one in whose breast such memories are all too few, he is all too richly repaid. If she does that, he is blessed indeed."

"She does. He is!" cried Winnifred, deeply moved. "Here on her knees she blesses him. And now," she added, "we must part. Seek not to follow me. One who has aided a poor girl in the hour of need will respect her wish when she tells him that, alone and buffeted by the world, her one prayer is that he will leave her."

"He will!" cried the Unknown. "He will. He does."

"Leave me, yes, leave me," exclaimed Winnifred.

"I will," said the Unknown.

"Do, do," sobbed the distraught girl. "Yet stay, one moment more. Let she, who has received so much from her benefactor, at least know his name."

"He cannot! He must not!" exclaimed the Indistinguishable. "His birth is such— but enough!"

He tore his hand from the girl's detaining clasp and rushed forth from the place.

Winnifred Clair was alone.

CHAPTER III

FRIENDS IN DISTRESS

WINNIFRED was now in the humblest lodgings in the humblest part of London. A simple bedroom and sitting-room sufficed for her wants. Here she sat on her trunk, bravely planning for the future.

"Miss Clair," said the Landlady, knocking at the door, "do try to eat something. You must keep up your health. See, I've brought you a kippered herring."

Winnifred ate the herring, her heart filled with gratitude. With renewed strength she sallied forth on the street to resume her vain search for employment. For two weeks now Winnifred Clair had sought employment even of the humblest character. At various dressmaking establishments she had offered, to no purpose, the services of her needle. They had looked at it and refused it.

In vain she had offered to various editors and publishers the use of her pen. They had examined it coldly and refused it.

She had tried fruitlessly to obtain a position of trust. The various banks and trust companies to which she had applied declined her services. In vain she had advertised in the newspapers offering to take sole charge of a little girl. No one would give her one.

Her slender stock of money which she had in her purse on leaving Mr. Bonehead's office was almost consumed.

Each night the unhappy girl returned to her lodging exhausted with disappointment and fatigue.

Yet even in her adversity she was not altogether friendless.

Each evening, on her return home, a soft tap was heard at the door.

"Miss Clair," said the voice of the Landlady, "I have brought you a fried egg. Eat it. You must keep up your strength."

Then one morning a terrible temptation had risen before her.

"Miss Clair," said the manager of an agency to which she had applied, "I am glad to be able at last to make you a definite offer of employment. Are you prepared to go upon the stage?"

The stage!

A flush of shame and indignation swept over the girl. Had it come to this? Little versed in the world as Winnifred was, she knew but too well the horror, the iniquity, the depth of degradation implied in the word.

"Yes," continued the agent, "I have a letter here asking me to recommend a young lady of suitable refinement to play the part of Eliza in *Uncle Tom's Cabin*. Will you accept?"

"Sir," said Winnifred proudly, "answer me first this question fairly. If I go upon the stage, can I, as Eliza, remain as innocent, as simple as I am now?"

"You can not," said the manager.

"Then, sir," said Winnifred, rising from her chair, "let me say this. Your offer is doubtless intended to be kind. Coming from the class you do, and inspired by the ideas you are, you no doubt mean well. But let a poor girl, friendless and alone, tell you that rather than accept such a degradation she will die."

"Very good," said the manager.

"I go forth," cried Winnifred, "to perish."

"All right," said the manager.

The door closed behind her. Winnifred Clair, once more upon the street, sank down upon the steps of the building in a swoon.

But at this very juncture Providence, which always watches over the innocent and defenceless, was keeping its eye direct upon Winnifred.

At that very moment when our heroine sank fainting upon the doorstep, a handsome equipage, drawn by two superb black steeds, happened to pass along the street.

Its appearance and character proclaimed it at once to be one of those vehicles in which only the superior classes of the exclusive aristocracy are privileged to ride. Its sides were emblazoned with escutcheons, insignia and other paraphernalia. The large gilt coronet that appeared up its panelling, surmounted by a bunch of huckleberries, quartered in a field of potatoes, indicated that its possessor was, at least, of the rank of marquis. A coachman and two grooms rode in front, while two footmen, seated in the boot, or box at the rear, contrived, by the immobility of their attitude and the melancholy of their faces, to inspire the scene with an exclusive and aristocratic grandeur.

The occupants of the equipage—for we refuse to count the menials as being such—were two in number, a lady and gentleman, both of advanced years. Their snow-white hair and benign countenances indicated that they belonged to that rare class of beings to whom rank and wealth are but an incentive to nobler things. A gentle philanthropy played all over their faces, and their eyes sought eagerly in the passing scene of the humble street for new objects of benefaction.

Those acquainted with the countenances of the aristocracy would have recognized at once in the occupants of the equipage the Marquis of Muddlenut and his spouse, the Marchioness.

It was the eye of the Marchioness which first detected the form of Winnifred Clair upon the doorstep.

"Hold ! pause ! stop !" she cried, in lively agitation.

The horses were at once pulled in, the brakes applied to the wheels, and with the aid of a powerful lever, operated by three of the menials, the carriage was brought to a standstill.

"See ! Look !" cried the Marchioness. "She has fainted. Quick, William, your flask. Let us hasten to her aid."

In another moment the noble lady was bending over the prostrate form of Winnifred Clair, and pouring brandy between her lips.

Winnifred opened her eyes. "Where am I ?" she asked feebly.

"She speaks !" cried the Marchioness. "Give her another flaskful."

After the second flask the girl sat up.

"Tell me," she cried, clasping her hands, "what has happened ? Where am I ?"

"With friends !" answered the Marchioness. "But do not essay to speak. Drink this. You must husband your strength. Meantime, let us drive you to your home."

Winnifred was lifted tenderly by the men-

23

servants into the aristocratic equipage. The brake was unset, the lever reversed, and the carriage thrown again into motion.

On the way Winnifred, at the solicitation of the Marchioness, related her story.

" My poor child ! " exclaimed the lady, " how you must have suffered. Thank Heaven it is over now. To-morrow we shall call for you and bring you away with us to Muddlenut Chase."

Alas, could she but have known it, before the morrow should dawn, worse dangers still were in store for our heroine. But what these dangers were, we must reserve for another chapter.

CHAPTER IV

A GAMBLING PARTY IN ST. JAMES'S CLOSE

WE must now ask our readers to shift the scene—if they don't mind doing this for us— to the apartments of the Earl of Wynchgate in St. James's Close. The hour is nine o'clock in the evening, and the picture before us is one

24

of revelry and dissipation so characteristic of the nobility of England. The atmosphere of the room is thick with blue Havana smoke such as is used by the nobility, while on the green baize table a litter of counters and cards, in which aces, kings, and even two spots are heaped in confusion, proclaim the reckless nature of the play.

Seated about the table are six men, dressed in the height of fashion, each with collar and white necktie and broad white shirt, their faces stamped with all, or nearly all, of the baser passions of mankind.

Lord Wynchgate—for he it was who sat at the head of the table—rose with an oath, and flung his cards upon the table.

All turned and looked at him, with an oath. "Curse it, Dogwood," he exclaimed, with another oath, to the man who sat beside him. "Take the money. I play no more to-night. My luck is out."

"Ha! ha!" laughed Lord Dogwood, with a third oath, "your mind is not on the cards. Who is the latest young beauty, pray, who so absorbs you ? I hear a whisper in town of a certain misadventure of yours——"

"Dogwood," said Wynchgate, clenching his fist, "have a care, man, or you shall measure the length of my sword."

Both noblemen faced each other, their hands upon their swords.

"My lords, my lords!" pleaded a distinguished-looking man of more advanced years, who sat at one side of the table, and in whose features the habitués of diplomatic circles would have recognized the handsome lineaments of the Marquis of Frogwater, British Ambassador to Siam, "let us have no quarrelling. Come, Wynchgate, come, Dogwood," he continued, with a mild oath, "put up your swords. It were a shame to waste time in private quarrelling. They may be needed all too soon in Cochin China, or, for the matter of that," he added sadly, "in Cambodia or in Dutch Guinea."

"Frogwater," said young Lord Dogwood, with a generous flush, "I was wrong. Wynchgate, your hand."

The two noblemen shook hands.

"My friends," said Lord Wynchgate, "in asking you to abandon our game, I had an end in view. I ask your help in an affair of the heart."

"Ha! excellent!" exclaimed the five noblemen. "We are with you heart and soul."

"I propose this night," continued Wynchgate, "with your help, to carry off a young girl, a female!"

"An abduction!" exclaimed the Ambassador somewhat sternly. "Wynchgate, I cannot countenance this."

"Mistake me not," said the Earl, "I intend to abduct her. But I propose nothing dishonourable. It is my firm resolve to offer her marriage."

"Then," said Lord Frogwater, "I am with you."

"Gentlemen," concluded Wynchgate, "all is ready. The coach is below. I have provided masks, pistols, and black cloaks. Follow me."

A few moments later, a coach, with the blinds drawn, in which were six noblemen armed to the teeth, might have been seen, were it not for the darkness, approaching the humble lodging in which Winnifred Clair was sheltered.

But what it did when it got there, we must leave to another chapter.

CHAPTER V

THE ABDUCTION

THE hour was twenty minutes to ten on the evening described in our last chapter.

Winnifred Clair was seated, still fully dressed, at the window of the bedroom, looking out over the great city.

A light tap came at the door.

"If it's a fried egg," called Winnifred softly, "I do not need it. I ate yesterday."

"No," said the voice of the Landlady. "You are wanted below."

"I!" exclaimed Winnifred, "below!"

"You," said the Landlady, "below. A party of gentlemen have called for you."

"Gentlemen," exclaimed Winnifred, putting her hand to her brow in perplexity, "for me! at

28

this late hour! Here! This evening! In this house?"

"Yes," repeated the Landlady, "six gentlemen. They arrived in a closed coach. They are all closely masked and heavily armed. They beg you will descend at once."

"Just Heaven!" cried the Unhappy Girl. "Is it possible that they mean to abduct me?"

"They do," said the Landlady. "They said so!"

"Alas!" cried Winnifred, "I am powerless. Tell them"—she hesitated—"tell them I will be down immediately. Let them not come up. Keep them below on any pretext. Show them an album. Let them look at the goldfish. Anything, but not here! I shall be ready in a moment."

Feverishly she made herself ready. As hastily as possible she removed all traces of tears from her face. She threw about her shoulders an opera cloak, and with a light Venetian scarf half concealed the beauty of her hair and features. "Abducted!" she murmured, "and by six of them! I think she said six. Oh, the horror of it!" A touch of powder to her cheeks and a slight blackening of her eyebrows, and the courageous girl was ready.

Lord Wynchgate and his companions—for they it was, that is to say, they were it—sat below in the sitting-room looking at the albums. "Woman," said Lord Wynchgate to the Landlady, with an oath, "let her hurry up. We have seen enough of these. We can wait no longer."

"I am here," cried a clear voice upon the threshold, and Winnifred stood before them. "My lords, for I divine who you are and wherefore you have come, take me, do your worst with me, but spare, oh, spare this humble companion of my sorrow."

"Right-oh!" said Lord Dogwood, with a brutal laugh.

"Enough," exclaimed Wynchgate, and seizing Winnifred by the waist, he dragged her forth out of the house and out upon the street.

But something in the brutal violence of his behaviour seemed to kindle for the moment a spark of manly feeling, if such there were, in the breasts of his companions.

"Wynchgate," cried young Lord Dogwood, "my mind misgives me. I doubt if this is a gentlemanly thing to do. I'll have no further hand in it."

A chorus of approval from his companions endorsed his utterance. For a moment they hesitated.

"Nay," cried Winnifred, turning to confront the masked faces that stood about her, "go forward with your fell design. I am here. I am helpless. Let no prayers stay your hand. Go to it."

"Have done with this!" cried Wynchgate, with a brutal oath. "Shove her in the coach."

But at the very moment the sound of hurrying footsteps was heard, and a clear, ringing, manly, well-toned, vibrating voice cried, "Hold! Stop! Desist! Have a care, titled villain, or I will strike you to the earth."

A tall aristocratic form bounded out of the darkness.

"Gentlemen," cried Wynchgate, releasing his hold upon the frightened girl, "we are betrayed. Save yourselves. To the coach."

31

In another instant the six noblemen had leaped into the coach and disappeared down the street.

Winnifred, still half inanimate with fright, turned to her rescuer, and saw before her the form and lineaments of the Unknown Stranger, who had thus twice stood between her and disaster. Half fainting, she fell swooning into his arms.

"Dear lady," he exclaimed, "rouse yourself. You are safe. Let me restore you to your home!"

"That voice!" cried Winnifred, resuming consciousness. "It is my benefactor."

She would have swooned again, but the Unknown lifted her bodily up the steps of her home and leant her against the door.

"Farewell," he said, in a voice resonant with gloom.

"Oh, sir!" cried the unhappy girl, "let one who owes so much to one who has saved her in her hour of need at least know his name."

But the stranger, with a mournful gesture

32

of farewell, had disappeared as rapidly as he had come.

But, as to why he had disappeared, we must ask our reader's patience for another chapter.

CHAPTER VI

THE UNKNOWN

THE scene is now shifted, sideways and forwards, so as to put it at Muddlenut Chase, and to make it a fortnight later than the events related in the last chapter.

Winnifred is now at the Chase as the guest of the Marquis and Marchioness. There her bruised soul finds peace.

The Chase itself was one of those typical country homes which are, or were till yesterday, the glory of England. The approach to the Chase lay through twenty miles of glorious forest, filled with fallow deer and wild bulls. The house itself, dating from the time of the Plantagenets, was surrounded by a moat covered with broad lilies and floating green scum. Magnificent peacocks sunned themselves

c   33

on the terraces, while from the surrounding shrubberies there rose the soft murmur of doves, pigeons, bats, owls and partridges.

Here sat Winnifred Clair day after day upon the terrace recovering her strength, under the tender solicitude of the Marchioness.

Each day the girl urged upon her noble hostess the necessity of her departure. "Nay," said the Marchioness, with gentle insistence, "stay where you are. Your soul is bruised. You must rest."

"Alas," cried Winnifred, "who am I that I should rest? Alone, despised, buffeted by fate, what right have I to your kindness?"

"Miss Clair," replied the noble lady, "wait till you are stronger. There is something that I wish to say to you."

Then at last, one morning when Winnifred's temperature had fallen to ninety-eight point three, the Marchioness spoke.

"Miss Clair," she said, in a voice which throbbed with emotion, "Winnifred, if I may so call you, Lord Muddlenut and I have formed a plan for your future. It is our dearest wish that you should marry our son."

"Alas," cried Winnifred, while tears rose in her eyes, "it cannot be!"

"Say not so," cried the Marchioness. "Our son, Lord Mordaunt Muddlenut, is young, handsome, all that a girl could desire. After months of wandering he returns to us this morning. It is our dearest wish to see him married and established. We offer you his hand."

"Indeed," replied Winnifred, while her tears fell even more freely, "I seem to requite but ill the kindness that you show. Alas, my heart is no longer in my keeping."

"Where is it?" cried the Marchioness.

"It is another's. One whose very name I do not know holds it in his keeping."

But at this moment a blithe, gladsome step was heard upon the flagstones of the terrace. A manly, ringing voice, which sent a thrill to Winnifred's heart, cried "Mother!" and in another instant Lord Mordaunt Muddlenut, for he it was, had folded the Marchioness to his heart.

35

Winnifred rose, her heart beating wildly. One glance was enough. The newcomer, Lord Mordaunt, was none other than the Unknown, the Unaccountable, to whose protection she had twice owed her life.

With a wild cry Winnifred Clair leaped across the flagstones of the terrace and fled into the park.

CHAPTER VII

THE PROPOSAL

THEY stood beneath the great trees of the ancestral park, into which Lord Mordaunt had followed Winnifred at a single bound. All about them was the radiance of early June.

Lord Mordaunt knelt on one knee on the greensward, and with a touch in which respect and reverence were mingled with the deepest and manliest emotion, he took between his finger and thumb the tip of the girl's gloved hand.

"Miss Clair," he uttered, in a voice suffused with the deepest yearning, yet vibrating with

36

the most profound respect, "Miss Clair—
Winnifred—hear me, I implore!"

"Alas," cried Winnifred, struggling in vain
to disengage the tip of her glove from the im-
petuous clasp of the young nobleman, "alas,
whither can I fly? I do not know my way
through the wood, and there are bulls in all
directions. I am not used to them! Lord
Mordaunt, I implore you, let the tears of
one but little skilled in the art of dissimula-
tion——"

"Nay, Winnifred," said the Young Earl,
"fly not. Hear me out!"

"Let me fly," begged the unhappy girl.

"You must not fly," pleaded Mordaunt.
"Let me first, here upon bended knee, convey
to you the expression of a devotion, a love, as
ardent and as deep as ever burned in a human
heart. Winnifred, be my bride!"

"Oh, sir," sobbed Winnifred, "if the knowledge of a gratitude, a thankfulness from one
whose heart will ever treasure as its proudest
memory the recollection of one who did for one
all that one could have wanted done for one—

if this be some poor guerdon, let it suffice. But, alas, my birth, the dark secret of my birth forbids——"

"Nay," cried Mordaunt, leaping now to his feet, "your birth is all right. I have looked into it myself. It is as good—or nearly as good—as my own. Till I knew this, my lips were sealed by duty. While I supposed that you had a lower birth and I an upper, I was bound to silence. But come with me to the house. There is one arrived with me who will explain all."

Hand in hand the lovers, for such they now were, returned to the Chase. There in the great hall the Marquis and the Marchioness were standing ready to greet them.

"My child!" exclaimed the noble lady, as she folded Winnifred to her heart. Then she turned to her son. "Let her know all!" she cried.

Lord Mordaunt stepped across the room to a curtain. He drew it aside, and there stepped forth Mr. Bonehead, the old lawyer who had cast Winnifred upon the world.

"Miss Clair," said the Lawyer, advancing and taking the girl's hand for a moment in a kindly clasp, "the time has come for me to explain all. You are not, you never were, the penniless girl that you suppose. Under the terms of your father's will, I was called upon to act a part and to throw you upon the world. It was my client's wish, and I followed it. I told you, quite truthfully, that I had put part of your money into options in an oil-well. Miss Clair, that well is now producing a million gallons of gasolene a month!'

"A million gallons!" cried Winnifred. "I can never use it."

"Wait till you own a motor-car, Miss Winnifred," said the Lawyer.

"Then I am rich!" exclaimed the bewildered girl.

"Rich beyond your dreams," answered the Lawyer. "Miss Clair, you own in your own right about half of the State of Texas—I think it is in Texas, at any rate either Texas or Rhode Island, or one of those big states in America. More than this, I have invested your property since your father's death so wisely that even after paying the income tax and the property tax, the inheritance tax, the dog tax and the tax on amusements, you will still have one half of one per cent to spend."

Winnifred clasped her hands.

"I knew it all the time," said Lord Mordaunt, drawing the girl to his embrace, "I found it out through this good man."

"We knew it too," said the Marchioness. "Can you forgive us, darling, our little plot for your welfare? Had we not done this Mordaunt might have had to follow you over to America and chase you all around Newport and Narragansett at a fearful expense."

"How can I thank you enough?" cried Winnifred. Then she added eagerly, "And my birth, my descent?"

"It is all right," interjected the Old Lawyer. "It is A 1. Your father, who died before you were born, quite a little time before, belonged to the very highest peerage of Wales. You are descended directly from Claer-ap-Claer, who murdered Owen Glendower. Your mother we are still tracing up. But we have already connected her with Floyd-ap-Floyd, who murdered Prince Llewellyn."

"Oh, sir," cried the grateful girl. "I only hope I may prove worthy of them!"

"One thing more," said Lord Mordaunt, and stepping over to another curtain he drew it aside and there emerged Lord Wynchgate.

He stood before Winnifred, a manly contrition struggling upon features which, but for the evil courses of he who wore them, might have been almost presentable.

"Miss Clair," he said, "I ask your pardon. I tried to carry you off. I never will again. But before we part let me say that my acquaintance with you has made me a better man, broader, bigger and, I hope, deeper."

With a profound bow, Lord Wynchgate took his leave.

CHAPTER VIII

WEDDED AT LAST

LORD MORDAUNT and his bride were married forthwith in the parish church of Muddlenut Chase. With Winnifred's money they have drained the moat, rebuilt the Chase, and chased the bulls out of the park. They have six children, so far, and are respected, honoured and revered in the countryside far and wide, over a radius of twenty miles in circumference.

II

JOHN AND I

OR, HOW I NEARLY LOST MY HUSBAND

(Narrated after the approved fashion of the best
Heart and Home Magazines)

II.—John and I; or, How I Nearly Lost My Husband

IT was after we had been married about two years that I began to feel that I needed more air. Every time I looked at John across the breakfast-table, I felt as if I must have more air, more space.

I seemed to feel as if I had no room to expand. I had begun to ask myself whether I had been wise in marrying John, whether John was really sufficient for my development. I felt cramped and shut in. In spite of myself the question would arise in my mind whether John really understood my nature. He had a way of reading the newspaper, propped up against the sugar - bowl, at breakfast, that somehow made me feel as if things had gone all wrong. It was bitter to realize that the time had come when John could prefer the newspaper to his wife's society.

45

But perhaps I had better go back and tell the whole miserable story from the beginning.

I shall never forget—I suppose no woman ever does—the evening when John first spoke out his love for me. I had felt for some time past that it was there. Again and again, he seemed about to speak. But somehow his words seemed to fail him. Twice I took him into the very heart of the little wood beside Mother's house, but it was only a small wood, and somehow he slipped out on the other side. "Oh, John," I had said, "how lonely and still it seems in the wood with no one here but ourselves! Do you think," I said, "that the birds have souls?" "I don't know," John answered, "let's get out of this." I was sure that his emotion was too strong for him. "I never feel a bit lonesome where you are, John," I said, as we made our way among the underbrush. "I think we can get out down that little gully," he answered. Then one evening in June after tea I led John down a path beside the house to a little corner behind the garden where there was a stone wall on one side and a high fence right in front of us, and thorn bushes on the other side. There was a little bench in the angle of the wall and the fence, and we sat down on it.

"Minnie," John said, "there's something I meant to say——"

"Oh, John," I cried, and I flung my arms round his neck. It all came with such a flood of surprise.

"All I meant, Minn——" John went on, but I checked him.

"Oh, don't, John, don't say anything more," I said. "It's just too perfect." Then I rose and seized him by the wrist. "Come," I said, "come to Mother," and I rushed him along the path.

As soon as Mother saw us come in hand in hand in this way, she guessed everything. She threw both her arms round John's neck and fairly pinned him against the wall. John tried to speak, but Mother wouldn't let him. "I saw it all along, John," she said. "Don't speak. Don't say a word. I guessed your love for Minn from the very start. I don't know what

47

I shall do without her, John, but she's yours now ; take her." Then Mother began to cry and I couldn't help crying too. "Take him to Father," Mother said, and we each took one of John's wrists and took him to Father on the back verandah. As soon as John saw Father he tried to speak again—"I think I ought to say," he began, but Mother stopped him. "Father," she said, "he wants to take our little girl away. He loves her very dearly, Alfred," she said, "and I think it our duty to let her go, no matter how hard it is, and oh, please Heaven, Alfred, he'll treat her well and not misuse her, or beat her," and she began to sob again.

Father got up and took John by the hand and shook it warmly.

"Take her, boy," he said. "She's all yours now, take her."

So John and I were engaged, and in due time our wedding day came and we were married. I remember that for days and days before the wedding day John seemed very nervous and depressed ; I think he was worrying, poor boy,

as to whether he could really make me happy
and whether he could fill my life as it should
be filled. But I told him that he was not
to worry, because I *meant* to be happy, and
was determined just to make the best of
everything.

Father stayed with John a good deal before
the wedding day, and on the wedding morning
he went and fetched him to the church in a
closed carriage and had him there all ready
when we came. It was a beautiful day in
September, and the church looked just lovely.
I had a beautiful gown of white organdie with
tulle at the throat, and I carried a great bunch
of white roses, and Father led John up the aisle
after me.

I remember that Mother cried a good deal
at the wedding, and told John that he had
stolen her darling and that he must never
misuse me or beat me. And I remember that
the clergyman spoke very severely to John, and
told him he hoped he realized the responsibility
he was taking and that it was his duty to make
me happy. A lot of our old friends were there,

and they all spoke quite sharply to John, and all the women kissed me and said they hoped I would never regret what I had done, and I just kept up my spirits by sheer determination, and told them that I had made up my mind to be happy and that I was going to be so.

So presently it was all over and we were driven to the station and got the afternoon train for New York, and when we sat down in the compartment among all our bandboxes and flowers, John said, "Well, thank God, that's over." And I said, "Oh, John, an oath! on our wedding day, an oath!" John said, "I'm sorry, Minn, I didn't mean——" but I said, "Don't, John, don't make it worse. Swear at me if you must, but don't make it harder to bear."

.   .   .   .   .

We spent our honeymoon in New York. At first I had thought of going somewhere to the great lonely woods, where I could have walked under the great trees and felt the silence of nature, and where John should have been my Viking and captured me with his spear, and where I should be his and his alone and no other man should share me; and John had said all right. Or else I had planned to go away somewhere to the seashore, where I could have watched the great waves dashing themselves against the rocks. I had told John that he should be my cave man, and should seize me in his arms and carry me whither he would. I felt somehow that for my development I wanted to get as close to nature as ever I could —that my mind seemed to be reaching out for a great emptiness. But I looked over all the hotel and steamship folders I could find and it seemed impossible to get good accommodation, so we came to New York. I had a great deal of shopping to do for our new house, so I could not be much with John, but I felt it was not right to neglect him, so I drove him somewhere in a taxi each morning and called for him again in the evening. One day I took him to the Metropolitan Museum, and another day I left him at the Zoo, and another day at the aquarium. John seemed very happy and quiet among the fishes.

So presently we came back home, and I spent many busy days in fixing and arranging our new house. I had the drawing-room done in blue, and the dining-room all in dark panelled wood, and a boudoir upstairs done in pink and white enamel to match my bedroom and dressing-room. There was a very nice little room in the basement next to the coal cellar that I turned into a " den " for John, so that when he wanted to smoke he could go down there and do it. John seemed to appreciate his den at once, and often would stay down there so long that I had to call to him to come up.

When I look back on those days they seem very bright and happy. But it was not very long before a change came. I began to realize that John was neglecting me. I noticed it at first in small things. I don't know just how long it was after our marriage that John began to read the newspaper at breakfast. At first he would only pick it up and read it in little bits, and only on the front page. I tried not to be hurt at it, and would go on talking just as brightly as I could, without seeming to notice anything. But presently he went on to reading the inside part of the paper, and then one day he opened up the financial page and folded the paper right back and leant it against the sugar-bowl.

I could not but wonder whether John's love for me was what it had been. Was it cooling? I asked myself. And what was cooling it? It hardly seemed possible, when I looked back to the wild passion with which he had proposed to me on the garden bench, that John's love was waning. But I kept noticing different little things. One day in the spring-time I saw John getting out a lot of fishing tackle from a box and fitting it together. I asked him what he was going to do, and he said that he was going to fish. I went to my room and had a good cry. It seemed dreadful that he could neglect his wife for a few worthless fish.

So I decided to put John to the test. It had been my habit every morning after he put his coat on to go to the office to let John have one kiss, just one weeny kiss, to keep him happy all day. So this day when he was getting ready I bent my head over a big bowl of flowers and pretended not to notice. I think John must have been hurt, as I heard him steal out on tiptoe.

Well, I realized that things had come to a dreadful state, and so I sent over to Mother, and Mother came, and we had a good cry together. I made up my mind to force myself to face things and just to be as bright as ever I could. Mother and I both thought that things would be better if I tried all I could to make something out of John. I have always felt that every woman should make all that she can out of her husband. So I did my best first of all to straighten up John's appearance. I shifted the style of collar he was wearing to a tighter kind that I liked better, and I brushed his hair straight backward instead of forward, which gave him a much more alert look. Mother said that John needed waking up, and so we did all we could to wake him up. Mother came over to stay with me a good deal, and in the evenings we generally had a little music or a game of cards.

About this time another difficulty began to come into my married life, which I suppose I ought to have foreseen—I mean the attentions of other gentlemen. I have always called forth a great deal of admiration in gentlemen, but I have always done my best to act like a lady and to discourage it in every possible way. I had been innocent enough to suppose that this would end with married life, and it gave me a dreadful shock to realize that such was not the case. The first one I noticed was a young man who came to the house, at an hour when John was out, for the purpose, so he said at least, of reading the gas meter. He looked at me in just the boldest way and asked me to show him the way to the cellar. I don't know whether it was a pretext or not, but I just summoned all the courage I had and showed him to the head of the cellar stairs. I had determined that if he tried to carry me down with him I would scream for the servants, but I suppose something in my manner made him desist, and he went alone. When he came up he professed to have read the meter and he left the house quite quietly. But I thought it wiser to say nothing to John of what had happened.

There were others too. There was a young man with large brown eyes who came and said he had been sent to tune the piano. He came on three separate days, and he bent his ear over the keys in such a mournful way that I knew he must have fallen in love with me. On the last day he offered to tune my harp for a dollar extra, but I refused, and when I asked him instead to tune Mother's mandoline he said he didn't know how. Of course I told John nothing of all this.

Then there was Mr. McQueen, who came to the house several times to play cribbage with John. He had been desperately in love with me years before—at least I remember his taking me home from a hockey match once, and what a struggle it was for him not to come into the parlour and see Mother for a few minutes when I asked him ; and, though he was married now and with three children, I felt sure when he came to play cribbage with John that it *meant* something. He was very discreet and honourable, and never betrayed himself for a moment, and I acted my part as if there was nothing at all behind. But one night, when he came over to play and John had had to go out, he refused to stay even for an instant. He had got his overshoes off before I told him that John was out, and asked him if he wouldn't come into the parlour and hear Mother play the mandoline, but he just made one dive for his overshoes and was gone. I knew that he didn't dare to trust himself.

Then presently a new trouble came. I began to suspect that John was drinking. I don't mean for a moment that he was drunk, or that he was openly cruel to me. But at times he seemed to act so queerly, and I noticed that one night when by accident I left a bottle of raspberry vinegar on the sideboard overnight, it was all gone in the morning. Two or three times when McQueen and John were to play cribbage, John would fetch home two or three bottles of bevo with him and they would sit sipping all evening.

I think he was drinking bevo by himself,

too, though I could never be sure of it. At any rate he often seemed queer and restless in the evenings, and instead of staying in his den he would wander all over the house. Once we heard him—I mean Mother and I and two lady friends who were with us that evening—quite late (after ten o'clock) apparently moving about in the pantry. "John," I called, "is that you?" "Yes, Minn," he answered, quietly enough, I admit. "What are you doing there?" I asked. "Looking for something to eat," he said. "John," I said, "you are forgetting what is due to me as your wife. You were fed at six. Go back."

He went. But yet I felt more and more that his love must be dwindling to make him act as he did. I thought it all over wearily enough and asked myself whether I had done everything I should to hold my husband's love. I had kept him in at nights. I had cut down his smoking. I had stopped his playing cards. What more was there that I could do?

.   .   .   .   .

So at last the conviction came to me that I

must go away. I felt that I must get away somewhere and think things out. At first I thought of Palm Beach, but the season had not opened and I felt somehow that I couldn't wait. I wanted to get away somewhere by myself and just face things as they were. So one morning I said to John, "John, I think I'd like to go off somewhere for a little time, just to be by myself, dear, and I don't want you to ask to come with me or to follow me, but just let me go." John said, "All right, Minn. When are you going to start?" The cold brutality of it cut me to the heart, and I went upstairs and had a good cry and looked over steamship and railroad folders. I thought of Havana for a while, because the pictures of the harbour and the castle and the queer Spanish streets looked so attractive, but then I was afraid that at Havana a woman alone by herself might be simply persecuted by attentions from gentlemen. They say the Spanish temperament is something fearful. So I decided on Bermuda instead. I felt that in a beautiful, quiet place like Bermuda I could think everything all over and face things, and it said on the folder that there were always at least two English regiments in garrison there, and the English officers, whatever their faults, always treat a woman with the deepest respect.

So I said nothing more to John, but in the next few days I got all my arrangements made and my things packed. And when the last afternoon came I sat down and wrote John a long letter, to leave on my boudoir table, telling him that I had gone to Bermuda. I told him that I wanted to be alone : I said that I couldn't tell when I would be back—that it might be months, or it might be years, and I hoped that he would try to be as happy as he could and forget me entirely, and to send me money on the first of every month.

. . . . .

Well, it was just at that moment that one of those strange coincidences happen, little things in themselves, but which seem to alter the whole course of a person's life. I had nearly finished the letter to John that I was to leave on the writing-desk, when just then the maid came up to my room with a telegram. It was for John, but I thought it my duty to open it and read it for him before I left. And I nearly fainted when I saw that it was from a lawyer in Bermuda—of all places—and it said that a legacy of two hundred thousand dollars had been left to John by an uncle of his who had died there, and asking for instructions about the disposition of it.

A great wave seemed to sweep over me, and all the wicked thoughts that had been in my mind—for I saw now that they *were* wicked—were driven clean away. I thought how completely lost poor old John would feel if all this money came to him and he didn't have to work any more and had no one at his side to help and guide him in using it.

I tore up the wicked letter I had written, and I hurried as fast as I could to pack up a valise with John's things (my own were packed already, as I said). Then presently John came in, and I broke the news to him as gently and as tenderly as I could about his uncle having left him the money and having died. I told him that I had found out all about the trains and the Bermuda steamer, and had everything all packed and ready for us to leave at once. John seemed a little dazed about it all, and kept saying that his uncle had taught him to play tennis when he was a little boy, and he was very grateful and thankful to me for having everything arranged, and thought it wonderful.

I had time to telephone to a few of my women friends, and they just managed to rush round for a few minutes to say good-bye. I couldn't help crying a little when I told them about John's uncle dying so far away with none of us near him, and I told them about the legacy, and they cried a little to hear of it all ; and when I told them that John and I might not come back direct from Bermuda, but might take a run over to Europe first, they all cried some more.

We left for New York that evening, and after we had been to Bermuda and arranged about a suitable monument for John's uncle and collected the money, we sailed for Europe.

All through the happy time that has followed, I like to think that through all our trials and difficulties affliction brought us safely together at last.

III

THE SPLIT IN THE CABINET

OR, THE FATE OF ENGLAND

(*A political novel of the Days that Were*)

E

III.—*The Split in the Cabinet; or, The Fate of England.*

CHAPTER I

"THE fate of England hangs upon it," murmured Sir John Elphinspoon, as he sank wearily into an armchair. For a moment, as he said "England," the baronet's eye glistened and his ears lifted as if in defiance, but as soon as he stopped saying it his eye lost its brilliance and his ears dropped wearily at the sides of his head.

Lady Elphinspoon looked at her husband anxiously. She could not conceal from herself that his face, as he sank into his chair, seemed somehow ten years older than it had been ten years ago.

"You are home early, John?" she queried.

"The House rose early, my dear," said the baronet.

" For the All England Ping - Pong match ? "

" No, for the Dog Show. The Prime Minister felt that the Cabinet ought to attend. He said that their presence there would help to bind the colonies to us. I understand also that he has a pup in the show himself. He took the Cabinet with him."

" And why not you ? " asked Lady Elphin-spoon.

" You forget, my dear," said the baronet, " as Foreign Secretary my presence at a Dog Show might be offensive to the Shah of Persia. Had it been a Cat Show——"

The baronet paused and shook his head in deep gloom.

" John," said his wife, " I feel that there is something more. Did anything happen at the House ? "

Sir John nodded.

" A bad business," he said. " The Wazu-chistan Boundary Bill was read this afternoon for the third time."

No woman in England, so it was generally

said, had a keener political insight than Lady Elphinspoon.

"The third time," she repeated thoughtfully, "and how many more will it have to go?"

Sir John turned his head aside and groaned.

"You are faint," exclaimed Lady Elphinspoon, "let me ring for tea."

The baronet shook his head.

"An egg, John—let me beat you up an egg."

"Yes, yes," murmured Sir John, still abstracted, "beat it, yes, do beat it."

Lady Elphinspoon, in spite of her elevated position as the wife of the Foreign Secretary of Great Britain, held it not beneath her to perform for her husband the plainest household service. She rang for an egg. The butler broke it for her into a tall goblet filled with old sherry, and the noble lady, with her own hands, beat the stuff out of it. For the veteran politician, whose official duties rarely allowed him to eat, an egg was a sovereign remedy. Taken either in a goblet of sherry or in a mug of rum, or in half a pint of whisky, it never failed to revive his energies.

69

The effect of the egg was at once visible in the brightening of his eye and the lengthening of his ears.

"And now explain to me," said his wife, "what has happened. What *is* this Boundary Bill?"

"We never meant it to pass," said Sir John. "It was introduced only as a sop to public opinion. It delimits our frontier in such a way as to extend our suzerainty over the entire desert of El Skrub. The Wazoos have claimed that this is their desert. The hill tribes are restless. If we attempt to advance the Wazoos will rise. If we retire it deals a blow at our prestige."

Lady Elphinspoon shuddered. Her long political training had taught her that nothing was so fatal to England as to be hit in the prestige.

"And on the other hand," continued Sir John, "if we move sideways, the Ohulîs, the mortal enemies of the Wazoos, will strike us in our rear."

"In our rear!" exclaimed Lady Elphinspoon in a tone of pain. "Oh, John, we must go forward. Take another egg."

"We cannot," groaned the Foreign Secretary. "There are reasons which I cannot explain even to you, Caroline, reasons of State, which absolutely prevent us from advancing into Wazuchistan. Our hands are tied. Meantime if the Wazoos rise, it is all over with us. It will split the Cabinet."

"Split the Cabinet!" repeated Lady Elphinspoon in alarm. She well knew that next to a blow in the prestige the splitting of the Cabinet was about the worst thing that could happen to Great Britain. "Oh, John, they *must* be held together at all costs. Can nothing be done?"

"Everything is being done that can be. The Prime Minister has them at the Dog Show at this moment. To-night the Chancellor is taking them to moving pictures. And to-morrow—it is a State secret, my dear, but it will be very generally known in the morning—we have seats for them all at the circus. If we can hold them together all is well, but if

71

they split we are undone. Meantime our difficulties increase. At the very passage of the
Bill itself a question was asked by one of the
new labour members, a miner, my dear, a quite
uneducated man——"

"Yes?" queried Lady Elphinspoon.

"He asked the Colonial Secretary"—Sir
John shuddered—"to tell him where Wazu-
chistan is. Worse than that, my dear," added
Sir John, "he defied him to tell him where it is."

"What did you do? Surely he has no right
to information of that sort?"

"It was a close shave. Luckily the Whips
saved us. They got the Secretary out of the
House and rushed him to the British Museum.
When he got back he said that he would answer
the question a month from Friday. We got
a great burst of cheers, but it was a close thing.
But stop, I must speak at once with Powers.
My despatch box, yes, here it is. Now where
is young Powers? There is work for him to
do at once."

"Mr. Powers is in the conservatory with
Angela," said Lady Elphinspoon.

"With Angela!" exclaimed Sir John, while a slight shade of displeasure appeared upon his brow. "With Angela again! Do you think it quite proper, my dear, that Powers should be so constantly with Angela?"

"John," said his wife, "you forget, I think, who Mr. Powers is. I am sure that Angela knows too well what is due to her rank, and to herself, to consider Mr. Powers anything more than an instructive companion. And I notice that, since Mr. Powers has been your secretary, Angela's mind is much keener. Already the girl has a wonderful grasp on foreign policy. Only yesterday I heard her asking the Prime Minister at luncheon whether we intend to extend our Senegambian protectorate over the Fusees. He was delighted."

"Oh, very well, very well," said Sir John. Then he rang a bell for a manservant.

"Ask Mr. Powers," he said, "to be good enough to attend me in the library."

CHAPTER II

ANGELA ELPHINSPOON stood with Perriton Powers among the begonias of the conservatory. The same news which had so agitated Sir John lay heavy on both their hearts.

"Will the Wazoo rise?" asked Angela, clasping her hands before her, while her great eyes sought the young man's face and found it. "Oh, Mr. Powers! Tell me, will they rise? It seems too dreadful to contemplate. Do you think the Wazoo will rise?"

"It is only too likely," said Powers. They stood looking into one another's eyes, their thoughts all on the Wazoo.

Angelina Elphinspoon, as she stood there against the background of the begonias, made a picture that a painter, or even a plumber, would have loved. Tall and typically English in her fair beauty, her features, in repose, had something of the hauteur and distinction of her mother, and when in motion they recalled her father.

Perriton Powers was even taller than Angela.

74

The splendid frame and stern features of Sir John's secretary made him a striking figure. Yet he was, quite frankly, sprung from the people, and made no secret of it. His father had been simply a well-to-do London surgeon, who had been knighted for some mere discoveries in science. His grandfather, so it was whispered, had been nothing more than a successful banker who had amassed a fortune simply by successful banking. Yet at Oxford young Powers had carried all before him. He had occupied a seat, a front seat, in one of the boats, had got his blue and his pink, and had taken a double final in Sanscrit and Arithmetic.

He had already travelled widely in the East, spoke Urdu and Hoodoo with facility, while as secretary to Sir John Elphinspoon, with a seat in the House in prospect, he had his foot upon the ladder of success.

"Yes," repeated Powers thoughtfully, "they may rise. Our confidential despatches tell us that for some time they have been secretly passing round packets of yeast. The whole tribe is in a ferment."

"But our sphere of influence is at stake," exclaimed Angela.

"It is," said Powers. "As a matter of fact, for over a year we have been living on a mere *modus vivendi*."

"Oh, Mr. Powers," cried Angela, "what a way to live."

"We have tried everything," said the secretary. "We offered the Wazoo a condominium over the desert of El Skrub. They refused it."

"But it's our desert," said Angela proudly.

"It is. But what can we do? The best we can hope is that El Boob will acquiesce in the *status quo*."

At that moment a manservant appeared in the doorway of the conservatory.

"Mr. Powers, sir," he said, "Sir John desires your attendance, sir, in the library, sir."

Powers turned to Angela, a new seriousness upon his face.

"Miss Elphinspoon," he said, "I think I know what is coming. Will you wait for me here? I shall be back in half an hour."

"I will wait," said the girl. She sat down

and waited among the begonias, her mind still on the Wazoo, her whole intense nature strung to the highest pitch. "Can the *modus vivendi* hold?" she murmured.

In half an hour Powers returned. He was wearing now his hat and light overcoat, and carried on a strap round his neck a tin box with a white painted label, "*British Foreign Office. Confidential Despatches. This Side Up With Care.*"

"Miss Elphinspoon," he said, and there was a new note in his voice, "Angela, I leave England to-night——"

"To-night!" gasped Angela.

"On a confidential mission."

"To Wazuchistan!" exclaimed the girl.

Powers paused a moment. "To Wazuchistan," he said, "yes. But it must not be known. I shall return in a month—or never. If I fail"—he spoke with an assumed lightness—"it is only one more grave among the hills. If I succeed, the Cabinet is saved, and with it the destiny of England."

"Oh, Mr. Powers," cried Angela, rising and

advancing towards him, "how splendid! How noble! No reward will be too great for you."

"My reward," said Powers, and as he spoke he reached out and clasped both of the girl's hands in his own, "yes, my reward. May I come and claim it here?"

For a moment he looked straight into her eyes. In the next he was gone, and Angela was alone.

"His reward!" she murmured. "What could he have meant? His reward that he is to claim. What can it be?"

But she could not divine it. She admitted to herself that she had not the faintest idea.

CHAPTER III

In the days that followed all England was thrilled to its base as the news spread that the Wazoo might rise at any moment.

"Will the Wazoos rise?" was the question upon every lip.

In London men went to their offices with a sense of gloom. At lunch they could hardly

78

eat. A feeling of impending disaster pervaded all ranks.

Sir John as he passed to and fro to the House was freely accosted in the streets.

"Will the Wazoos rise, sir?" asked an honest labourer. "Lord help us all, sir, if they do."

Sir John, deeply touched, dropped a shilling in the honest fellow's hat, by accident.

At No. 10 Downing Street, women of the working class, with children in their arms, stood waiting for news.

On the Exchange all was excitement. Consols fell two points in twenty-four hours. Even raising the Bank rate and shutting the door brought only a temporary relief.

Lord Glump, the greatest financial expert in London, was reported as saying that if the Wazoos rose England would be bankrupt in forty-eight hours.

Meanwhile, to the consternation of the whole nation, the Government did nothing. The Cabinet seemed to be paralysed.

On the other hand the Press became all the

more clamorous. The London *Times* urged that an expedition should be sent at once. Twenty-five thousand household troops, it argued, should be sent up the Euphrates or up the Ganges or up something without delay. If they were taken in flat boats, carried over the mountains on mules, and lifted across the rivers in slings, they could then be carried over the desert on jackasses. They could reach Wazuchistan in two years. Other papers counselled moderation. The *Manchester Guardian* recalled the fact that the Wazoos were a Christian people. Their leader, El Boob, so it was said, had accepted Christianity with childlike simplicity and had asked if there was any more of it. The *Spectator* claimed that the Wazoos, or more properly the Wazi, were probably the descendants of an Iranic or perhaps Urgumic stock. It suggested the award of a Rhodes Scholarship. It looked forward to the days when there would be Wazoos at Oxford. Even the presence of a single Wazoo, or, more accurately, a single Wooz, would help.

With each day the news became more ominous. It was reported in the Press that a Wazoo, inflamed apparently with *ghee*, or perhaps with *bhong*, had rushed up to the hills and refused to come down. It was said that the Shriek-ul-Foozlum, the religious head of the tribe, had torn off his suspenders and sent them to Mecca.

That same day the *Illustrated London News* published a drawing "Wazoo Warriors Crossing a River and Shouting, Ho!" and the general consternation reached its height.

Meantime, for Sir John and his colleagues, the question of the hour became, "Could the Cabinet be held together?" Every effort was made. The news that the Cabinet had all been seen together at the circus, for a moment reassured the nation. But the rumour spread that the First Lord of the Admiralty had said that the clowns were a bum lot. The Radical Press claimed that if he thought so he ought to resign.

On the fatal Friday the question already

referred to was scheduled for its answer. The friends of the Government counted on the answer to restore confidence. To the consternation of all, the expected answer was not forthcoming. The Colonial Secretary rose in his place, visibly nervous. Ministers, he said, had been asked where Wazuchistan was. They were not prepared, at the present delicate stage of negotiations, to say. More hung upon the answer than Ministers were entitled to divulge. They could only appeal to the patriotism of the nation. He could only say this, that *wherever* it was, and he used the word *wherever* with all the emphasis of which he was capable, the Government would accept the full responsibility for its being where it was.

The House adjourned in something like confusion.

Among those seated behind the grating of the Ladies' Gallery was Lady Elphinspoon. Her quick instinct told her the truth. Driving home, she found her husband seated, crushed, in his library.

"John," she said, falling on her knees and

taking her husband's hands in hers, " is this true ? Is this the dreadful truth ? "

" I see you have divined it, Caroline," said the statesman sadly. " It is the truth. We don't know where Wazuchistan is."

For a moment there was silence.

" But, John, how could it have happened ? "

" We thought the Colonial Office knew. We were confident that they knew. The Colonial Secretary had stated that he had been there. Later on it turned out that he meant Saskatchewan. Of course they thought *we* knew. And we both thought that the Exchequer must know. We understood that they had collected a hut tax for ten years."

" And hadn't they ? "

" Not a penny. The Wazoos live in tents."

" But, surely," pleaded Lady Elphinspoon, " you could find out. Had you no maps ? "

Sir John shook his head.

" We thought of that at once, my dear. We've looked all through the British Museum. Once we thought we had succeeded. But it turned out to be Wisconsin."

83

"But the map in the *Times?* Everybody saw it."

Again the baronet shook his head. "Lord Southcliff had it made in the office," he said. "It appears that he always does. Otherwise the physical features might not suit him."

"But could you not send some one to see?"

"We did. We sent Perriton Powers to find out where it was. We had a month to the good. It was barely time, just time. Powers has failed and we are lost. To-morrow all England will guess the truth and the Government falls."

CHAPTER IV

THE crowd outside of No. 10 Downing Street that evening was so dense that all traffic was at a standstill. But within the historic room where the Cabinet were seated about the long table all was calm. Few could have guessed from the quiet demeanour of the group of statesmen that the fate of an Empire hung by a thread.

84

Seated at the head of the table, the Prime Minister was quietly looking over a book of butterflies, while waiting for the conference to begin. Beside him the Secretary for Ireland was fixing trout flies, while the Chancellor of the Exchequer kept his serene face bent over upon his needlework. At the Prime Minister's right, Sir John Elphinspoon, no longer agitated, but sustained and dignified by the responsibility of his office, was playing spillikins.

The little clock on the mantel chimed eight.

The Premier closed his book of butterflies.

" Well, gentlemen," he said, " I fear our meeting will not be a protracted one. It seems we are hopelessly at variance. You, Sir Charles," he continued, turning to the First Sea Lord, who was in attendance, " are still in favour of a naval expedition ? "

" Send it up at once," said Sir Charles.

" Up where ? " asked the Premier.

" Up anything," answered the Old Sea Dog, " it will get there."

Voices of dissent were raised in undertones around the table.

"I strongly deprecate any expedition," said the Chancellor of the Exchequer, "I favour a convention with the Shriek. Let the Shriek sign a convention recognizing the existence of a supreme being and receiving from us a million sterling in acknowledgment."

"And where will you *find* the Shriek?" said the Prime Minister. "Come, come, gentlemen, I fear that we can play this comedy no longer. The truth is," he added with characteristic nonchalance, "we don't know where the bally place is. We can't meet the House to-morrow. We are hopelessly split. Our existence as a Government is at an end."

But, at that very moment, a great noise of shouting and clamour rose from the street without. The Prime Minister lifted his hand for silence. "Listen," he said. One of the Ministers went to a window and opened it, and the cries outside became audible. "A King's Messenger! Make way for the King's Messenger!"

The Premier turned quietly to Sir John.

"Perriton Powers," he said.

In another moment Perriton Powers stood before the Ministers.

Bronzed by the tropic sun, his face was recognizable only by the assured glance of his eye. An Afghan *bernous* was thrown back from his head and shoulders, while his commanding figure was draped in a long *chibuok*. A pair of pistols and a curved *yasmak* were in his belt.

"So you got to Wazuchistan all right," said the Premier quietly.

"I went in by way of the Barooda," said Powers. "For many days I was unable to cross it. The waters the river were wild and swollen with rains. To cross it seemed certain death——"

"But at last you got over," said the Premier, "and then——"

"I struck out over the Fahuri desert. For days and days, blinded by the sun, and almost buried in sand, I despaired."

"But you got through it all right. And after that?"

"My first care was to disguise myself.

87

Staining myself from head to foot with betel nut——"

" To look like a beetle," said the Premier. " Exactly. And so you got to Wazuchistan. Where is it and what is it ? "

" My lord," said Powers, drawing himself up and speaking with emphasis, " I got to where it was thought to be. There is no such place ! "

The whole Cabinet gave a start of astonishment.

" No such place ! " they repeated.

" What about El Boob ? " asked the Chancellor.

" There is no such person."

" And the Shriek-el-Foozlum ? "

Powers shook his head.

" But do you mean to say," said the Premier in astonishment, " that there are no Wazoos ? There you *must* be wrong. True we don't just know where they are. But our despatches have shown too many signs of active trouble traced directly to the Wazoos to disbelieve in them. There are Wazoos somewhere, there —there *must* be."

"The Wazoos," said Powers, "are there. But they are Irish. So are the Ohulîs. They are both Irish."

"But how the devil did they get out there?" questioned the Premier. "And why did they make the trouble?"

"The Irish, my lord," interrupted the Chief Secretary for Ireland, "are everywhere, and it is their business to make trouble."

"Some years ago," continued Powers, "a few Irish families settled out there. The Ohulîs should be properly called the O'Hooleys. The word Wazoo is simply the Urdu for McGinnis. El Boob is the Urdu for the Arabic El Papa, the Pope. It was my knowledge of Urdu, itself an agglutinative language——"

"Precisely," said the Premier. Then he turned to his Cabinet. "Well, gentlemen, our task is now simplified. If they are Irish, I think we know exactly what to do. I suppose," he continued, turning to Powers, "that they want some kind of Home Rule."

"They do," said Powers.

" Separating, of course, the Ohulî counties from the Wazoo ? "

" Yes," said Powers.

" Precisely ; the thing is simplicity itself. And what contribution will they make to the Imperial Exchequer ? "

" None."

" And will they pay their own expenses ? "

" They refuse to."

" Exactly. All this is plain sailing. Of course they must have a constabulary. Lord Edward," continued the Premier, turning now to the Secretary of War, " how long will it take to send in a couple of hundred constabulary ? I think they'll expect it, you know. It's their right."

" Let me see," said Lord Edward, calculating quickly, with military precision, " sending them over the Barooda in buckets and then over the mountains in baskets—I think in about two weeks."

" Good," said the Premier. " Gentlemen, we shall meet the House to-morrow. Sir John, will you meantime draft us an annexation bill ?

And you, young man, what you have done is really not half bad. His Majesty will see you to-morrow. I am glad that you are safe."

"On my way home," said Powers, with quiet modesty, "I was attacked by a lion——"

"But you beat it off," said the Premier. "Exactly. Good night."

CHAPTER V

I<small>T</small> was on the following afternoon that Sir John Elphinspoon presented the Wazoo Annexation Bill to a crowded and breathless House.

Those who know the House of Commons know that it has its moods. At times it is grave, earnest, thoughtful. At other times it is swept with emotion which comes at it in waves. Or at times, again, it just seems to sit there as if it were stuffed.

But all agreed that they had never seen the House so hushed as when Sir John Elphinspoon presented his Bill for the Annexation of

Wazuchistan. And when at the close of a splendid peroration he turned to pay a graceful compliment to the man who had saved the nation, and thundered forth to the delighted ears of his listeners—

Arma virumque cano Wazoo qui primus ab oris,

and then, with the words " England, England," still on his lips, fell over backwards and was carried out on a stretcher, the House broke into wild and unrestrained applause.

CHAPTER VI

THE next day Sir Perriton Powers—for the King had knighted him after breakfast—stood again in the conservatory of the house in Carlton Terrace.

" I have come for my reward," he said. " Do I get it ? "

" You do," said Angela.

WHO DO YOU THINK DID IT?

OR, THE MIXED-UP MURDER MYSTERY

(Done after the very latest fashion in this sort of thing)

IV.—Who Do You Think Did It? or, The Mixed-Up Murder Mystery

NOTE.—*Any reader who guesses correctly who did it is entitled (in all fairness) to a beautiful gold watch and chain.*

CHAPTER I

HE DINED WITH ME LAST NIGHT

THE afternoon edition of the *Metropolitan Planet* was going to press. Five thousand copies a minute were reeling off its giant cylinders. A square acre of paper was passing through its presses every hour. In the huge *Planet* building, which dominated Broadway, employés, compositors, reporters, advertisers, surged to and fro. Placed in a single line (only, of course, they wouldn't be likely to consent to it) they would have reached across Manhattan Island. Placed in two lines, they would probably have reached twice as far. Arranged in a procession they would have taken an hour in passing a saloon : easily that.

In the whole vast building all was uproar. Telephones, megaphones and gramophones were ringing throughout the building. Elevators flew up and down, stopping nowhere.

Only in one place was quiet—namely, in the room where sat the big man on whose capacious intellect the whole organization depended.

Masterman Throgton, the general manager of the *Planet*, was a man in middle life. There was something in his massive frame which suggested massiveness, and a certain quality in the poise of his great head which indicated a balanced intellect. His face was impenetrable and his expression imponderable.

The big chief was sitting in his swivel chair with ink all round him. Through this man's great brain passed all the threads and filaments that held the news of a continent. Snap one, and the whole continent would stop.

At the moment when our story opens (there was no sense in opening it sooner), a written message had just been handed in.

The Chief read it. He seemed to grasp its contents in a flash.

"Good God!" he exclaimed. It was the strongest expression that this solid, self-contained, semi-detached man ever allowed himself. Anything stronger would have seemed too near to profanity. "Good God!" he repeated, "Kivas Kelly murdered! In his own home! Why, he dined with me last night! I drove him home!"

For a brief moment the big man remained plunged in thought. But with Throgton the moment of musing was short. His instinct was to act.

"You may go," he said to the messenger. Then he seized the telephone that stood beside him (this man could telephone almost without stopping thinking) and spoke into it in quiet, measured tones, without wasting a word.

"Hullo, operator! Put me through to two, two, two, two, two. Is that two, two, two,

two, two? Hullo, two, two, two, two, two; I want Transome Kent. Kent speaking? Kent, this is Throgton speaking. Kent, a murder has been committed at the Kelly residence, Riverside Drive. I want you to go and cover it. Get it all. Don't spare expense. The *Planet* is behind you. Have you got car-fare? Right."

In another moment the big chief had turned round in his swivel chair (at least forty degrees) and was reading telegraphic despatches from Jerusalem. That was the way he did things.

CHAPTER II

I MUST SAVE HER LIFE

WITHIN a few minutes Transome Kent had leapt into a car (a surface car) and was speeding north towards Riverside Drive with the full power of the car. As he passed uptown a newsboy was already calling, "Club Man Murdered! Another Club Man Murdered!" Carelessly throwing a cent to the boy, Kent

purchased a paper and read the brief notice of
the tragedy.

Kivas Kelly, a well-known club man and *bon
vivant*, had been found dead in his residence
on Riverside Drive, with every indication——or,
at least, with a whole lot of indications——of
murder. The unhappy club man had been
found, fully dressed in his evening clothes, lying
on his back on the floor of the billiard-room,
with his feet stuck up on the edge of the table.
A narrow black scarf, presumably his evening
tie, was twisted tightly about his neck by means
of a billiard cue inserted in it. There was a
quiet smile upon his face. He had apparently
died from strangulation. A couple of bullet-
holes passed through his body, one on each side,
but they went out again. His suspenders were
burst at the back. His hands were folded
across his chest. One of them still held a
white billiard ball. There was no sign of a
struggle or of any disturbance in the room. A
square piece of cloth was missing from the
victim's dinner jacket.

In its editorial columns the same paper discussed the more general aspects of the murder. This, it said, was the third club man murdered in the last fortnight. While not taking an alarmist view, the paper felt that the killing of club men had got to stop. There was a limit, a reasonable limit, to everything. Why should a club man be killed? It might be asked, why should a club man live? But this was hardly to the point. They do live. After all, to be fair, what does a club man ask of society? Not much. Merely wine, women and singing. Why not let him have them? Is it fair to kill him? Does the gain to literature outweigh the social wrong? The writer estimated that at the rate of killing now going on the club men would be all destroyed in another generation. Something should be done to conserve them.

Transome Kent was not a detective. He was a reporter. After sweeping everything at Harvard in front of him, and then behind him, he had joined the staff of the *Planet* two months before. His rise had been phenomenal. In his first week of work he had unravelled a mystery, in his second he had unearthed a packing scandal which had poisoned the food of the entire nation for ten years, and in his third he had pitilessly exposed some of the best and most respectable people in the metropolis. Kent's work on the *Planet* consisted now almost exclusively of unravelling and unearthing, and it was natural that the manager should turn to him.

The mansion was a handsome sandstone residence, standing in its own grounds. On Kent's arrival he found that the police had already drawn a cordon around it with cords. Groups of morbid curiosity-seekers hung about it in twos and threes, some of them in fours and fives. Policemen were leaning against the fence in all directions. They wore that baffled look so common to the detective force of the metropolis. " It seems to me," remarked one of them to the man beside him, " that there is an inexorable chain of logic about this that I am unable to follow." " So do I," said the other.

The Chief Inspector of the Detective Department, a large, heavy-looking man, was standing beside a gate-post. He nodded gloomily to Transome Kent.

"Are you baffled, Edwards?" asked Kent.

"Baffled again, Mr. Kent," said the Inspector, with a sob in his voice. "I thought I could have solved this one, but I can't."

He passed a handkerchief across his eyes.

"Have a cigar, Chief," said Kent, "and let me hear what the trouble is."

The Inspector brightened. Like all policemen, he was simply crazy over cigars. "All right, Mr. Kent," he said, "wait till I chase away the morbid curiosity-seekers."

He threw a stick at them.

"Now, then," continued Kent, "what about tracks, footmarks? Had you thought of them?"

"Yes, first thing. The whole lawn is covered with them, all stamped down. Look at these, for instance. These are the tracks of a man with a wooden leg"—Kent nodded— "in all probability a sailor, newly landed from Java, carrying a Singapore walking-stick, and with a tin-whistle tied round his belt."

"Yes, I see that," said Kent thoughtfully.

"The weight of the whistle weighs him down a little on the right side."

"Do you think, Mr. Kent, a sailor from Java with a wooden leg would commit a murder like this?" asked the Inspector eagerly. "Would he do it?"

"He would," said the Investigator. "They generally do—as soon as they land."

The Inspector nodded. "And look at these marks here, Mr. Kent. You recognize them, surely—those are the footsteps of a bar-keeper out of employment, waiting for the eighteenth amendment to pass away. See how deeply they sink in——"

"Yes," said Kent, "he'd commit murder."

"There are lots more," continued the Inspector, "but they're no good. The morbid curiosity-seekers were walking all over this place while we were drawing the cordon round it."

"Stop a bit," said Kent, pausing to think a moment. "What about thumb-prints?"

"Thumb-prints," said the Inspector. "Don't mention them. The house is full of them."

"Any thumb-prints of Italians with that peculiar incurvature of the ball of the thumb that denotes a Sicilian brigand?"

"There were three of those," said Inspector Edwards gloomily. "No, Mr. Kent, the thumb stuff is no good."

Kent thought again.

"Inspector," he said, "what about mysterious women? Have you seen any around?"

"Four went by this morning," said the Inspector, "one at eleven-thirty, one at twelve-thirty, and two together at one-thirty. At least," he added sadly, "I think they were mysterious. All women look mysterious to me."

"I must try in another direction," said Kent. "Let me reconstruct the whole thing. I must weave a chain of analysis. Kivas Kelly was a bachelor, was he not?"

"He was. He lived alone here."

"Very good. I suppose he had in his employ a butler who had been with him for twenty years——"

Edwards nodded.

" I suppose you've arrested him ? "

" At once," said the Inspector. " We always arrest the butler, Mr. Kent. They expect it. In fact, this man, Williams, gave himself up at once."

" And let me see," continued the Investigator. " I presume there was a housekeeper who lived on the top floor, and who had been stone deaf for ten years ? "

" Precisely."

" She had heard nothing during the murder ? "

" Not a thing. But this may have been on account of her deafness."

" True, true," murmured Kent. " And I suppose there was a coachman, a thoroughly reliable man, who lived with his wife at the back of the house——"

" But who had taken his wife over to see a relation on the night of the murder, and who did not return until an advanced hour. Mr. Kent, we've been all over that. There's nothing in it."

" Were there any other persons belonging to the establishment ? "

"There was Mr. Kelly's stenographer, Alice Delary, but she only came in the mornings."

"Have you seen her?" asked Kent eagerly. "What is she like?"

"I have seen her," said the Inspector. "She's a looloo."

"Ha," said Kent, "a looloo!" The two men looked into one another's eyes.

"Yes," repeated Edwards thoughtfully, "a peach."

A sudden swift flash of intuition, an inspiration, leapt into the young reporter's brain.

This girl, this peach, at all hazards he must save her life.

CHAPTER III

I MUST BUY A BOOK ON BILLIARDS

KENT turned to the Inspector. "Take me into the house," he said. Edwards led the way. The interior of the handsome mansion seemed undisturbed. "I see no sign of a struggle here," said Kent.

108

"No," answered the Inspector gloomily. "We can find no sign of a struggle anywhere. But, then, we never do."

He opened for the moment the door of the stately drawing-room. "No sign of a struggle there," he said. The closed blinds, the draped furniture, the covered piano, the muffled chandelier, showed absolutely no sign of a struggle.

"Come upstairs to the billiard-room," said Edwards. "The body has been removed for the inquest, but nothing else is disturbed."

They went upstairs. On the second floor was the billiard-room, with a great English table in the centre of it. But Kent had at once dashed across to the window, an exclamation on his lips. "Ha! ha!" he said, "what have we here?"

The Inspector shook his head quietly. "The window," he said in a monotonous, almost sing-song tone, "has apparently been opened from the outside, the sash being lifted with some kind of a sharp instrument. The dust on the sill outside has been disturbed as if by a man of extraordinary agility lying on his stomach—— Don't bother about that, Mr. Kent. It's *always* there."

"True," said Kent. Then he cast his eyes upward, and again an involuntary exclamation broke from him. "Did you see that trap-door?" he asked.

"We did," said Edwards. "The dust around the rim has been disturbed. The trap opens into the hollow of the roof. A man of extraordinary dexterity might open the trap with a billiard cue, throw up a fine manila rope, climb up the rope and lie there on his stomach.

"No use," continued the Inspector. "For the matter of that, look at this huge old-fashioned fireplace. A man of extraordinary precocity could climb up the chimney. Or this dumb-waiter on a pulley, for serving drinks, leading down into the maids' quarters. A man of extreme indelicacy might ride up and down in it."

"Stop a minute," said Kent. "What is the meaning of that hat?"

A light gossamer hat, gay with flowers, hung on a peg at the side of the room.

"We thought of that," said Edwards, "and we have left it there. Whoever comes for that hat has had a hand in the mystery. We think——"

But Transome Kent was no longer listening. He had seized the edge of the billiard table.

"Look, look!" he cried eagerly. "The clue to the mystery! The positions of the billiard balls! The white ball in the very centre of the table, and the red just standing on the verge of the end pocket! What does it mean, Edwards, what does it mean?"

He had grasped Edwards by the arm and was peering into his face.

"I don't know," said the Inspector. "I don't play billiards."

"Neither do I," said Kent, "but I can find out. Quick! The nearest book-store. I must buy a book on billiards."

With a wave of the arm, Kent vanished.

The Inspector stood for a moment in thought.

"Gone!" he murmured to himself (it was his habit to murmur all really important speeches aloud to himself). "Now, why did Throgton telephone to me to put a watch on Kent? Ten dollars a day to shadow him! Why?"

CHAPTER IV

THAT IS NOT BILLIARD CHALK

MEANTIME at the *Planet* office Masterman Throgton was putting on his coat to go home.

"Excuse me, sir," said an employé, "there's a lot of green billiard chalk on your sleeve."

Throgton turned and looked the man full in the eye.

"That is not billiard chalk," he said, "it is face powder."

Saying which this big, imperturbable, self-contained man stepped into the elevator and went to the ground floor in one drop.

CHAPTER V

HAS ANYBODY HERE SEEN KELLY?

THE inquest upon the body of Kivas Kelly was held upon the following day. Far from offering any solution of what had now become an unfathomable mystery, it only made it deeper still. The medical testimony, though given by the most distinguished consulting expert of the city, was entirely inconclusive. The body, the expert testified, showed evident marks of violence. There was a distinct lesion of the œsophagus and a decided excoriation of the fibula. The mesodenum was gibbous. There was a certain quantity of flab in the binomium and the proscenium was wide open.

One striking fact, however, was decided from the testimony of the expert, namely, that the stomach of the deceased was found to contain half a pint of arsenic. On this point the questioning of the district attorney was close and technical. Was it unusual, he asked, to find arsenic in the stomach? In the stomach

H   113

of a club man, no. Was not half a pint a large quantity? He would not say that. Was it a small quantity? He should not care to say that it was. Would half a pint of arsenic cause death? Of a club man, no, not necessarily. That was all.

The other testimony submitted to the inquest jury brought out various facts of a substantive character, but calculated rather to complicate than to unravel the mystery. The butler swore that on the very day of the murder he had served his master a half-pint of arsenic at lunch. But he claimed that this was quite a usual happening with his master. On cross-examination it appeared that he meant apollinaris. He was certain, however, that it was half a pint. The butler, it was shown, had been in Kivas Kelly's employ for twenty years.

The coachman, an Irishman, was closely questioned. He had been in Mr. Kelly's employ for three years—ever since his arrival from the old country. Was it true that he had had, on the day of the murder, a violent quarrel with his master? It was. Had he threatened to kill him? No. He had threatened to knock his block off, but not to kill him.

The coroner looked at his notes. "Call Alice Delary," he commanded. There was a deep sensation in the court as Miss Delary quietly stepped forward to her place in the witness-box.

Tall, graceful and willowy, Alice Delary was in her first burst of womanhood. Those who looked at the beautiful girl realized that if her first burst was like this, what would the second, or the third be like?

The girl was trembling, and evidently distressed, but she gave her evidence in a clear, sweet, low voice. She had been in Mr. Kelly's employ three years. She was his stenographer. But she came only in the mornings and always left at lunch-time. The question immediately asked by the jury—"Where did she generally have lunch?"—was disallowed by the coroner. Asked by a member of the jury what system of shorthand she used, she answered, "Pitman's." Asked by another juryman whether she ever cared to go to moving pictures, she said that she went occasionally. This created a favourable impression. "Miss Delary," said the district attorney, "I want to ask if it is your hat that was found hanging in the billiard-room after the crime?"

"Don't you dare ask that girl that," interrupted the magistrate. "Miss Delary, you may step down."

But the principal sensation of the day arose out of the evidence offered by Masterman Throgton, general manager of the *Planet*. Kivas Kelly, he testified, had dined with him at his club on the fateful evening. He had afterwards driven him to his home.

"When you went into the house with the deceased," asked the district attorney, "how long did you remain there with him?"

"That," said Throgton quietly, "I must refuse to answer."

"Would it incriminate you?" asked the coroner, leaning forward.

"It might," said Throgton.

"Then you're perfectly right not to answer

it," said the coroner. "Don't ask him that any more. Ask something else."

"Then did you," questioned the attorney, turning to Throgton again, "play a game of billiards with the deceased?"

"Stop, stop," said the coroner, "that question I can't allow. It's too direct, too brutal; there's something about that question, something mean, dirty. Ask another."

"Very good," said the attorney. "Then tell me, Mr. Throgton, if you ever saw this blue envelope before?" He held up in his hand a long blue envelope.

"Never in my life," said Throgton.

"Of course he didn't," said the coroner. "Let's have a look at it. What is it?"

"This envelope, your Honour, was found sticking out of the waistcoat pocket of the deceased."

"You don't say," said the coroner. "And what's in it?"

Amid breathless silence, the attorney drew forth a sheet of blue paper, bearing a stamp, and read:

117

"This is the last will and testament of me, Kivas Kelly of New York. I leave everything of which I die possessed to my nephew, Peter Kelly."

The entire room gasped. No one spoke. The coroner looked all around. "Has anybody here seen Kelly?" he asked.

There was no answer.

The coroner repeated the question.

No one moved.

"Mr. Coroner," said the attorney, "it is my opinion that if Peter Kelly is found the mystery is fathomed."

Ten minutes later the jury returned a verdict of murder against a person or persons unknown, adding that they would bet a dollar that Kelly did it.

The coroner ordered the butler to be released, and directed the issue of a warrant for the arrest of Peter Kelly.

CHAPTER VI

SHOW ME THE MAN WHO WORE THOSE BOOTS

THE remains of the unhappy club man were buried on the following day as reverently as those of a club man can be. None followed him to the grave except a few morbid curiosity-seekers, who rode on top of the hearse.

The great city turned again to its usual avocations. The unfathomable mystery was dismissed from the public mind.

Meantime Transome Kent was on the trail. Sleepless, almost foodless, and absolutely drinkless, he was everywhere. He was looking for Peter Kelly. Wherever crowds were gathered, the Investigator was there, searching for Kelly. In the great concourse of the Grand Central Station, Kent moved to and fro, peering into everybody's face. An official touched him on the shoulder. "Stop peering into the people's faces," he said. "I am unravelling a mystery," Kent answered. "I beg your pardon, sir," said the man, "I didn't know."

Kent was here, and everywhere, moving ceaselessly, pro and con, watching for Kelly. For hours he stood beside the soda‑water fountains examining every drinker as he drank. For three days he sat on the steps of Master‑man Throgton's home, disguised as a plumber waiting for a wrench.

But still no trace of Peter Kelly. Young Kelly, it appeared, had lived with his uncle until a little less than three years ago. Then suddenly he had disappeared. He had vanished, as a brilliant writer for the New York Press framed it, as if the earth had swallowed him up.

Transome Kent, however, was not a man to be baffled by initial defeat.

A week later, the Investigator called in at the office of Inspector Edwards.

"Inspector," he said, "I must have some more clues. Take me again to the Kelly residence. I must re-analyse my first diær‑esis."

Together the two friends went to the house. "It is inevitable," said Kent, as they entered again the fateful billiard-room, "that we have overlooked something."

"We always do," said Edwards gloomily.

"Now tell me," said Kent, as they stood beside the billiard table, "what is your own theory, the police theory, of this murder? Give me your first theory first, and then go on with the others."

"Our first theory, Mr. Kent, was that the murder was committed by a sailor with a wooden leg, newly landed from Java."

"Quite so, quite proper," nodded Kent.

"We knew that he was a sailor," the Inspector went on, dropping again into his sing-song monotone, "by the extraordinary agility needed to climb up the thirty feet of bare brick wall to the window—a landsman could not have climbed more than twenty; the fact that he was from the East Indies we knew from the peculiar knot about his victim's neck. We knew that he had a wooden leg——"

The Inspector paused and looked troubled.

"We knew it." He paused again. "I'm afraid I can't remember that one."

"Tut, tut," said Kent gently, "you knew it, Edwards, because when he leaned against the billiard table the impress of his hand on the mahogany was deeper on one side than the other. The man was obviously top heavy. But you abandoned this first theory."

"Certainly, Mr. Kent, we always do. Our second theory was———"

But Kent had ceased to listen. He had suddenly stooped down and picked up something off the floor.

"Ha ha!" he exclaimed. "What do you make of this?" He held up a square fragment of black cloth.

"We never saw it," said Edwards.

"Cloth," muttered Kent, "the missing piece of Kivas Kelly's dinner jacket." He whipped out a magnifying glass. "Look," he said, "it's been stamped upon—by a man wearing hobnailed boots—made in Ireland—a man of five feet nine and a half inches high———"

"One minute, Mr. Kent," interrupted the Inspector, greatly excited, "I don't quite get it."

"The depth of the dint proves the lift of

his foot," said Kent impatiently, "and the lift of the foot indicates at once the man's height. Edwards, find me the man who wore these boots and the mystery is solved!"

At that very moment a heavy step, unmistakably to the trained ear that of a man in hob-nailed boots, was heard upon the stair. The door opened and a man stood hesitating in the doorway.

Both Kent and Edwards gave a start, two starts, of surprise.

The man was exactly five feet nine and a half inches high. He was dressed in coachman's dress. His face was saturnine and evil.

It was Dennis, the coachman of the murdered man.

"If you're Mr. Kent," he said, "there's a lady here asking for you."

CHAPTER VII

OH, MR. KENT, SAVE ME!

In another moment an absolutely noiseless step was heard upon the stair.

A young girl entered, a girl, tall, willowy and beautiful, in the first burst, or just about the first burst, of womanhood.

It was Alice Delary.

She was dressed with extreme taste, but Kent's quick eye noted at once that she wore no hat.

"Mr. Kent," she cried, "you are Mr. Kent, are you not? They told me that you were here. Oh, Mr. Kent, help me, save me!"

She seemed to shudder into herself a moment. Her breath came and went quickly.

She reached out her two hands.

"Calm yourself, my dear young lady," said Kent, taking them. "Don't let your breath come and go so much. Trust me. Tell me all."

"Mr. Kent," said Delary, regaining her control, but still trembling, "I want my hat."

Kent let go the beautiful girl's hands. "Sit down," he said. Then he went across the room and fetched the hat, the light gossamer hat, with flowers in it, that still hung on a peg.

"Oh, I am so glad to get it back," cried the

girl. " I can never thank you enough. I was afraid to come for it."

" It is all right," said the Inspector. " The police theory was that it was the housekeeper's hat. You are welcome to it."

Kent had been looking closely at the girl before him.

" You have more to say than that," he said. " Tell me all."

" Oh, I will, I will, Mr. Kent. That dreadful night! I was here. I saw, at least I heard it all."

She shuddered.

" Oh, Mr. Kent, it was dreadful! I had come back that evening to the library to finish some work. I knew that Mr. Kelly was to dine out and that I would be alone. I had been working quietly for some time when I became aware of voices in the billiard-room. I tried not to listen, but they seemed to be quarrelling, and I couldn't help hearing. Oh, Mr. Kent, was I wrong?"

" No," said Kent, taking her hand a moment, " you were not."

"I heard one say, 'Get your foot off the table, you've no right to put your foot on the table.' Then the other said, 'Well, you keep your stomach off the cushion then.'" The girl shivered. "Then presently one said, quite fiercely, 'Get back into balk there, get back fifteen inches,' and the other voice said, 'By God! I'll shoot from here.' Then there was a dead stillness, and then a voice almost screamed, 'You've potted me. You've potted me. That ends it.' And then I heard the other say in a low tone, 'Forgive me, I didn't mean it. I never meant it to end that way.'

"I was so frightened, Mr. Kent, I couldn't stay any longer. I rushed downstairs and ran all the way home. Then next day I read what had happened, and I knew that I had left my hat there, and was afraid. Oh, Mr. Kent, save me!"

"Miss Delary," said the Investigator, taking again the girl's hands and looking into her eyes, "you are safe. Tell me only one thing. The man who played against Kivas Kelly— did you see him?"

"Only for one moment"—the girl paused—
"through the keyhole."

"What was he like?" asked Kent. "Had he an impenetrable face?"

"He had."

"Was there anything massive about his face?"

"Oh, yes, yes, it was all massive."

"Miss Delary," said Kent, "this mystery is now on the brink of solution. When I have joined the last links of the chain, may I come and tell you all?"

She looked full in his face.

"At any hour of the day or night," she said, "you may come."

Then she was gone.

CHAPTER VIII

YOU ARE PETER KELLY

WITHIN a few moments Kent was at the phone.

"I want four, four, four, four. Is that four,

four, four, four ? Mr. Throgton's house ? I
want Mr. Throgton. Mr. Throgton speaking ?
Mr. Throgton, Kent speaking. The Riverside
mystery is solved."

Kent waited in silence a moment. Then
he heard Throgton's voice—not a note in it
disturbed :

" Has anybody found Kelly ? "

" Mr. Throgton," said Kent, and he spoke
with a strange meaning in his tone, " the story
is a long one. Suppose I relate it to you "—he
paused, and laid a peculiar emphasis on what
followed—" *over a game of billiards.*"

" What the devil do you mean ? " answered
Throgton.

" Let me come round to your house and tell
the story. There are points in it that I can
best illustrate over a billiard table. Suppose
I challenge you to a fifty point game before I
tell my story."

.   .   .   .   .

It required no little hardihood to challenge
Masterman Throgton at billiards. His reputation at his club as a cool, determined player

was surpassed by few. Throgton had been known to run nine, ten, and even twelve at a break. It was not unusual for him to drive his ball clear off the table. His keen eye told him infallibly where each of the three balls was ; instinctively he knew which to shoot with.

In Kent, however, he had no mean adversary. The young reporter, though he had never played before, had studied his book to some purpose. His strategy was admirable. Keeping his ball well under the shelter of the cushion, he eluded every stroke of his adversary, and in his turn caused his ball to leap or dart across the table with such speed as to bury itself in the pocket at the side.

The score advanced rapidly, both players standing precisely equal. At the end of the first half-hour it stood at ten all. Throgton, a grim look upon his face, had settled down to work, playing with one knee on the table. Kent, calm but alive with excitement, leaned well forward to his stroke, his eye held within an inch of the ball.

At fifteen they were still even. Throgton

I 129

with a sudden effort forced a break of three ; but Kent rallied and in another twenty minutes they were even again at nineteen all.

But it was soon clear that Transome Kent had something else in mind than to win the game. Presently his opportunity came. With a masterly stroke, such as few trained players could use, he had potted his adversary's ball. The red ball was left over the very jaws of the pocket. The white was in the centre.

Kent looked into Throgton's face.

The balls were standing in the very same position on the table as on the night of the murder.

" I did that on purpose," said Kent quietly.

" What do you mean ? " asked Throgton.

" The position of those balls," said Kent. " Mr. Throgton, come into the library. I have something to say to you. You know already what it is."

They went into the library. Throgton, his hand unsteady, lighted a cigar.

" Well," he said, " what is it ? "

" Mr. Throgton," said Kent, " two weeks ago

you gave me a mystery to solve. To-night I can give you the solution. Do you want it?"

Throgton's face never moved.

"Well," he said.

"A man's life," Kent went on, "may be played out on a billiard table. A man's soul, Throgton, may be pocketed."

"What devil's foolery is this?" said Throgton. "What do you mean?"

"I mean that your crime is known—plotter, schemer that you are, you are found out—hypocrite, traitor; yes, Masterman Throgton, or rather—let me give you your true name—*Peter Kelly*, murderer, I denounce you!"

Throgton never flinched. He walked across to where Kent stood, and with his open palm he slapped him over the mouth.

"Transome Kent," he said, "you're a liar."

Then he walked back to his chair and sat down.

"Kent," he continued, "from the first moment of your mock investigation, I knew who you were. Your every step was shadowed, your every movement dogged. Transome

131

Kent—by your true name, *Peter Kelly*, murderer, I denounce you."

Kent walked quietly across to Throgton and dealt him a fearful blow behind the ear.

" You're a liar," he said, " I am not Peter Kelly."

They sat looking at one another.

At that moment Throgton's servant appeared at the door.

" A gentleman to see you, sir."

" Who?" said Throgton.

" I don't know, sir, he gave his card."

Masterman Throgton took the card.

On it was printed :

PETER KELLY

CHAPTER IX

LET ME TELL YOU THE STORY OF MY LIFE

For a moment Throgton and Kent sat looking at one another.

"Show the man up," said Throgton.

A minute later the door opened and a man

entered. Kent's keen eye analysed him as he stood. His blue clothes, his tanned face, and the extraordinary dexterity of his fingers left no doubt of his calling. He was a sailor.

"Sit down," said Throgton.

"Thank you," said the sailor, "it rests my wooden leg."

The two men looked again. One of the sailor's legs was made of wood. With a start Kent noticed that it was made of East Indian sandalwood.

"I've just come from Java," said Kelly quietly, as he sat down.

Kent nodded. "I see it all now," he said. "Throgton, I wronged you. We should have known it was a sailor with a wooden leg from Java. There is no other way."

"Gentlemen," said Peter Kelly, "I've come to make my confession. It is the usual and right thing to do, gentlemen, and I want to go through with it while I can."

"One moment," said Kent, "do you mind interrupting yourself with a hacking cough?"

133

"Thank you, sir," said Kelly, "I'll get to that a little later. Let me begin by telling you the story of my life."

"No, no," urged Throgton and Kent, "don't do that!"

Kelly frowned. "I think I have a right to," he said. "You've got to hear it. As a boy I had a wild, impulsive nature. Had it been curbed——"

"But it wasn't," said Throgton. "What next?"

"I was the sole relative of my uncle, and heir to great wealth. Pampered with every luxury, I was on a footing of——"

"One minute," interrupted Kent, rapidly analysing as he listened. "How many legs had you then?"

"Two—on a footing of ease and indolence. I soon lost——"

"Your leg," said Throgton. "Mr. Kelly, pray come to the essential things."

"I will," said the sailor. "Gentlemen, bad as I was, I was not altogether bad."

"Of course not," said Kent and Throgton

134

soothingly. "Probably not more than ninety per cent."

"Even into my life, gentlemen, love entered. If you had seen her you would have known that she is as innocent as the driven snow. Three years ago she came to my uncle's house. I loved her. One day, hardly knowing what I was doing, I took her——" he paused.

"Yes, yes," said Throgton and Kent, "you took her?"

"To the Aquarium. My uncle heard of it. There was a violent quarrel. He disinherited me and drove me from the house. I had a liking for the sea from a boy."

"Excuse me," said Kent, "from what boy?"

Kelly went right on. "I ran away as a sailor before the mast."

"Pardon me," interrupted Kent, "I am not used to sea terms. Why didn't you run *behina* the mast?"

"Hear me out," said Kelly, "I am nearly done. We sailed for the East Indies—for Java. There a Malay pirate bit off my leg. I returned home, bitter, disillusioned, the mere wreck that you see. I had but one thought. I meant to kill my uncle."

For a moment a hacking cough interrupted Kelly. Kent and Throgton nodded quietly to one another.

"I came to his house at night. With the aid of my wooden leg I scaled the wall, lifted the window and entered the billiard-room. There was murder in my heart. Thank God I was spared from that. At the very moment when I got in, a light was turned on in the room and I saw before me—but no, I will not name her—my better angel. 'Peter!' she cried, then with a woman's intuition she exclaimed, 'You have come to murder your uncle. Don't do it.' My whole mood changed. I broke down and cried like a—like a——"

Kelly paused a moment.

"Like a boob," said Kent softly. "Go on."

"When I had done crying, we heard voices. 'Quick,' she exclaimed, 'flee, hide, he must not see you.' She rushed into the adjoining room, closing the door. My eye had noticed already

136

the trap above. I climbed up to it. Shall I explain how?"

"Don't," said Kent, "I can analyse it afterwards."

"There I saw what passed. I saw Mr. Throgton and Kivas Kelly come in. I watched their game. They were greatly excited and quarrelled over it. Throgton lost."

The big man nodded with a scowl. "By his potting the white," he said.

"Precisely," said Kelly, "he missed the red. Your analysis was wrong, Mr. Kent. The game ended. You started your reasoning from a false diæresis. In billiards people never mark the last point. The board still showed ninety-nine all. Throgton left and my uncle, as often happens, kept trying over the last shot —a half-ball shot, sir, with the red over the pocket. He tried again and again. He couldn't make it. He tried various ways. His rest was too unsteady. Finally he made his tie into a long loop round his neck and put his cue through it. 'Now, by gad!' he said, 'I can do it.'"

"Ha!" said Kent. "Fool that I was."

"Exactly," continued Kelly. "In the excitement of watching my uncle I forgot where I was, I leaned too far over and fell out of the trap. I landed on uncle, just as he was sitting on the table to shoot. He fell."

"I see it all!" said Kent. "He hit his head, the loop tightened, the cue spun round and he was dead."

"That's it," said Kelly. "I saw that he was dead, and I did not dare to remain. I straightened the knot in his tie, laid his hands reverently across his chest, and departed as I had come."

"Mr. Kelly," said Throgton thoughtfully, "the logic of your story is wonderful. It exceeds anything in its line that I have seen published for months. But there is just one point that I fail to grasp. The two bullet holes?"

"They were old ones," answered the sailor quietly. "My uncle in his youth had led a wild life in the west; he was full of them."

There was silence for a moment. Then Kelly spoke again:

"My time, gentlemen, is short." (A hacking cough interrupted him.) "I feel that I am withering. It rests with you, gentlemen, whether or not I walk out of this room a free man."

Transome Kent rose and walked over to the sailor.

"Mr. Kelly," he said, "here is my hand."

CHAPTER X

SO DO I

A FEW days after the events last narrated, Transome Kent called at the boarding-house of Miss Alice Delary. The young Investigator wore a light grey tweed suit, with a salmon-coloured geranium in his buttonhole. There was something exultant yet at the same time grave in his expression, as of one who has taken a momentous decision, affecting his future life.

"I wonder," he murmured, "whether I am acting for my happiness."

139

He sat down for a moment on the stone steps and analysed himself.

Then he rose.

"I am," he said, and rang the bell.

"Miss Delary?" said a maid, "she left here two days ago. If you are Mr. Kent, the note on the mantelpiece is for you."

Without a word (Kent never wasted them) the Investigator opened the note and read:

"DEAR MR. KENT,

"Peter and I were married yesterday morning, and have taken an apartment in Java, New Jersey. You will be glad to hear that Peter's cough is ever so much better. The lawyers have given Peter his money without the least demur.

"We both feel that your analysis was simply wonderful. Peter says he doesn't know where he would be without it.

"Very sincerely,

"ALICE KELLY.

"P.S.—I forgot to mention to you that I

saw Peter in the billiard-room.   But your
analysis was marvellous just the same."

.   .   .   .   .

That evening Kent sat with Throgton talking
over the details of the tragedy.

"Throgton," he said, "it has occurred to me
that there were points about that solution that
we didn't get exactly straight somehow."

"So do I," said Throgton.

V

BROKEN BARRIERS

OR, RED LOVE ON A BLUE ISLAND

(The kind of thing that has replaced the good Old Sea Story)

V.—*Broken Barriers; or, Red Love on a Blue Island.*

IT was on a bright August afternoon that I stepped on board the steamer *Patagonia* at Southampton outward bound for the West Indies and the Port of New Orleans.

I had at the time no presentiment of disaster. I remember remarking to the ship's purser, as my things were being carried to my state-room, that I had never in all my travels entered upon any voyage with so little premonition of accident. " Very good, Mr. Borus," he answered. " You will find your state-room in the starboard aisle on the right." I distinctly recall remarking to the Captain that I had never, in any of my numerous seafarings, seen the sea of a more limpid blue. He agreed with me so entirely,

K   145

as I recollect it, that he did not even trouble to answer.

Had anyone told me on that bright summer afternoon that our ship would within a week be wrecked among the Dry Tortugas, I should have laughed. Had anyone informed me that I should find myself alone on a raft in the Caribbean Sea, I should have gone into hysterics.

We had hardly entered the waters of the Caribbean when a storm of unprecedented violence broke upon us. Even the Captain had never, so he said, seen anything to compare with it. For two days and nights we encountered and endured the full fury of the sea. Our soup plates were secured with racks and covered with lids. In the smoking-room our glasses had to be set in brackets, and as our steward came and went, we were from moment to moment in imminent danger of seeing him washed overboard.

On the third morning just after daybreak the ship collided with something, probably either a floating rock or one of the dry Tortugas. She blew out her four funnels, the bowsprit dropped out of its place, and the propeller came right off. The Captain, after a brief consultation, decided to abandon her. The boats were lowered, and, the sea being now quite calm, the passengers were emptied into them.

By what accident I was left behind I cannot tell. I had been talking to the second mate and telling him of a rather similar experience of mine in the China Sea, and holding him by the coat as I did so, when quite suddenly he took me by the shoulders, and rushing me into the deserted smoking-room said, "Sit there, Mr. Borus, till I come back for you." The fellow spoke in such a menacing way that I thought it wiser to comply.

When I came out they were all gone. By good fortune I found one of the ship's rafts still lying on the deck. I gathered together such articles as might be of use and contrived, though how I do not know, to launch it into the sea.

On my second morning on my raft I was sitting quietly polishing my boots and talking to myself when I became aware of an object

147

floating in the sea close beside the raft. Judge
of my feelings when I realized it to be the
inanimate body of a girl. Hastily finishing
my boots and stopping talking to myself, I
made shift as best I could to draw the unhappy
girl towards me with a hook.

After several ineffectual attempts I at last
managed to obtain a hold of the girl's clothing
and drew her on to the raft.

She was still unconscious. The heavy life-
belt round her person must (so I divined) have
kept her afloat after the wreck. Her clothes
were sodden, so I reasoned, with the sea-water.

On a handkerchief which was still sticking
into the belt of her dress, I could see letters
embroidered. Realizing that this was no time
for hesitation, and that the girl's life might
depend on my reading her name, I plucked
it forth. It was Edith Croyden.

As vigorously as I could I now set to work
to rub her hands. My idea was (partly) to restore her circulation. I next removed her boots,
which were now rendered useless, as I argued,
by the sea-water, and began to rub her feet.

148

I was just considering what to remove next, when the girl opened her eyes. "Stop rubbing my feet," she said.

"Miss Croyden," I said, "you mistake me."

I rose, with a sense of pique which I did not trouble to conceal, and walked to the other end of the raft. I turned my back upon the girl and stood looking out upon the leaden waters of the Caribbean Sea. The ocean was now calm. There was nothing in sight.

I was still searching the horizon when I heard a soft footstep on the raft behind me, and a light hand was laid upon my shoulder. "Forgive me," said the girl's voice.

I turned about. Miss Croyden was standing behind me. She had, so I argued, removed her stockings and was standing in her bare feet. There is something, I am free to confess, about a woman in her bare feet which hits me where I live. With instinctive feminine taste the girl had twined a piece of seaweed in her hair. Seaweed, as a rule, gets me every time. But I checked myself.

149

"Miss Croyden," I said, "there is nothing to forgive."

At the mention of her name the girl blushed for a moment and seemed about to say something, but stopped.

"Where are we?" she queried presently.

"I don't know," I answered, as cheerily as I could, "but I am going to find out."

"How brave you are!" Miss Croyden exclaimed.

"Not at all," I said, putting as much heartiness into my voice as I was able to.

The girl watched my preparations with interest.

With the aid of a bent pin hoisted on a long pole I had no difficulty in ascertaining our latitude.

"Miss Croydon," I said, "I am now about to ascertain our longitude. To do this I must lower myself down into the sea. Pray do not be alarmed or anxious. I shall soon be back."

With the help of a long line I lowered myself deep down into the sea until I was enabled to ascertain, approximately at any rate, our longitude. A fierce thrill went through me at the thought that this longitude was our longitude, hers and mine. On the way up, hand over hand, I observed a long shark looking at me. Realizing that the fellow if voracious might prove dangerous, I lost but little time—indeed, I may say I lost absolutely no time—in coming up the rope.

The girl was waiting for me.

"Oh, I am so glad you have come back," she exclaimed, clasping her hands.

"It was nothing," I said, wiping the water from my ears, and speaking as melodiously as I could.

"Have you found our whereabouts?" she asked.

"Yes," I answered. "Our latitude is normal, but our longitude is, I fear, at least three degrees out of the plumb. I am afraid, Miss Croyden," I added, speaking as mournfully as I knew how, "that you must reconcile your mind to spending a few days with me on this raft."

" Is it as bad as that ? " she murmured, her eyes upon the sea.

In the long day that followed, I busied myself as much as I could with my work upon the raft, so as to leave the girl as far as possible to herself. It was, so I argued, absolutely necessary to let her feel that she was safe in my keeping. Otherwise she might jump off the raft and I should lose her.

I sorted out my various cans and tins, tested the oil in my chronometer, arranged in neat order my various ropes and apparatus, and got my frying-pan into readiness for any emergency. Of food we had for the present no lack.

With the approach of night I realized that it was necessary to make arrangements for the girl's comfort. With the aid of a couple of upright poles I stretched a grey blanket across the raft so as to make a complete partition.

" Miss Croyden," I said, " this end of the raft is yours. Here you may sleep in peace."

" How kind you are," the girl murmured.

" You will be quite safe from interference,"

I added. "I give you my word that I will not obtrude upon you in any way."

"How chivalrous you are," she said.

"Not at all," I answered, as musically as I could. "Understand me, I am now putting my head over this partition for the last time. If there is anything you want, say so now."

"Nothing," she answered.

"There is a candle and matches beside you. If there is anything that you want in the night, call me instantly. Remember, at any hour I shall be here. I promise it."

"Good night," she murmured. In a few minutes her soft regular breathing told me that she was asleep.

I went forward and seated myself in a tar-bucket, with my head against the mast, to get what sleep I could.

But for some time—why, I do not know—sleep would not come.

The image of Edith Croyden filled my mind. In vain I told myself that she was a stranger to me : that—beyond her longitude—I knew nothing of her. In some strange way this girl had seized hold of me and dominated my senses.

The night was very calm and still, with great stars in a velvet sky. In the darkness I could hear the water lapping the edge of the raft.

I remained thus in deep thought, sinking further and further into the tar-bucket. By the time I reached the bottom of it I realized that I was in love with Edith Croyden.

Then the thought of my wife occurred to me and perplexed me. Our unhappy marriage had taken place three years before. We brought to one another youth, wealth and position. Yet our marriage was a failure. My wife—for what reason I cannot guess—seemed to find my society irksome. In vain I tried to interest her with narratives of my travels. They seemed—in some way that I could not divine —to fatigue her. " Leave me for a little, Harold," she would say (I forgot to mention that my name is Harold Borus), " I have a pain in my neck." At her own suggestion I had taken a trip around the world. On my return she urged me to go round again. I was going

round for the third time when the wrecking of
the steamer had interrupted my trip.

On my own part, too, I am free to confess
that my wife's attitude had aroused in me a
sense of pique, not to say injustice. I am not
in any way a vain man. Yet her attitude
wounded me. I would no sooner begin,
"When I was in the Himalayas hunting the
humpo or humped buffalo," than she would
interrupt and say, "Oh, Harold, would you
mind going down to the billiard-room and
seeing if I left my cigarettes under the
billiard-table?" When I returned, she was
gone.

By agreement we had arranged for a divorce.
On my completion of my third voyage we were
to meet in New Orleans. Clara was to go
there on a separate ship, giving me the choice
of oceans.

Had I met Edith Croyden three months
later I should have been a man free to woo
and win her. As it was I was bound. I must
put a clasp of iron on my feelings. I must
wear a mask. Cheerful, helpful, and full of

narrative, I must yet let fall no word of love to this defenceless girl.

After a great struggle I rose at last from the tar-bucket, feeling, if not a brighter, at least a cleaner man.

Dawn was already breaking. I looked about me. As the sudden beams of the tropic sun illumined the placid sea, I saw immediately before me, only a hundred yards away, an island. A sandy beach sloped back to a rocky eminence, broken with scrub and jungle. I could see a little stream leaping among the rocks. With eager haste I paddled the raft close to the shore till it ground in about ten inches of water.

I leaped into the water.

With the aid of a stout line, I soon made the raft fast to a rock. Then as I turned I saw that Miss Croyden was standing upon the raft, fully dressed, and gazing at me. The morning sunlight played in her hair, and her deep blue eyes were as soft as the Caribbean Sea itself.

"Don't attempt to wade ashore, Miss Croyden," I cried in agitation. "Pray do nothing rash. The waters are simply infested with bacilli."

"But how can I get ashore?" she asked, with a smile which showed all, or nearly all, of her pearl-like teeth.

"Miss Croyden," I said, "there is only one way. I must carry you."

In another moment I had walked back to the raft and lifted her as tenderly and reverently as if she had been my sister—indeed more so— in my arms.

Her weight seemed nothing. When I get a girl like that in my arms I simply don't feel it. Just for one moment as I clasped her thus in my arms, a fierce thrill ran through me. But I let it run.

When I had carried her well up the sand close to the little stream, I set her down. To my surprise, she sank down in a limp heap.

The girl had fainted.

I knew that it was no time for hesitation.

Running to the stream, I filled my hat with water and dashed it in her face. Then I took up a handful of mud and threw it at her with all my force. After that I beat her with my hat.

At length she opened her eyes and sat up.

" I must have fainted," she said, with a little shiver. " I am cold. Oh, if we could only have a fire."

" I will do my best to make one, Miss Croyden," I replied, speaking as gymnastically as I could. " I will see what I can do with two dry sticks."

" With dry sticks ? " queried the girl. " Can you light a fire with that ? How wonderful you are ! "

" I have often seen it done," I replied thoughtfully ; " when I was hunting the humpo, or humped buffalo, in the Himalayas, it was our usual method."

" Have you really hunted the humpo ? " she asked, her eyes large with interest.

" I have indeed," I said, " but you must rest ; later on I will tell you about it."

" I wish you could tell me now," she said with a little moan.

Meantime I had managed to select from the driftwood on the beach two sticks that seemed absolutely dry. Placing them carefully together, in Indian fashion, I then struck a match and found no difficulty in setting them on fire.

In a few moments the girl was warming herself beside a generous fire.

Together we breakfasted upon the beach beside the fire, discussing our plans like comrades.

Our meal over, I rose.

"I will leave you here a little," I said, "while I explore."

With no great difficulty I made my way through the scrub and climbed the eminence of tumbled rocks that shut in the view.

On my return Miss Croyden was still seated by the fire, her head in her hands.

"Miss Croyden," I said, "we are on an island."

"Is it inhabited?" she asked.

"Once, perhaps, but not now. It is one of the many keys of the West Indies. Here, in old buccaneering days, the pirates landed and careened their ships."

"How did they do that?" she asked, fascinated.

"I am not sure," I answered. "I think with white-wash. At any rate, they gave them a good careening. But since then these solitudes are only the home of the sea-gull, the sea-mew, and the albatross."

The girl shuddered.

"How lonely!" she said.

"Lonely or not," I said with a laugh (luckily I can speak with a laugh when I want to), "I must get to work."

I set myself to work to haul up and arrange our effects. With a few stones I made a rude table and seats. I took care to laugh and sing as much as possible while at my work. The close of the day found me still busy with my labours.

"Miss Croyden," I said, "I must now arrange a place for you to sleep."

With the aid of four stakes driven deeply into the ground and with blankets strung upon them, I managed to fashion a sort of rude tent, roofless, but otherwise quite sheltered.

"Miss Croyden," I said when all was done, "go in there."

Then, with little straps which I had fastened to the blankets, I buckled her in reverently.

"Good night, Miss Croyden," I said.

"But you," she exclaimed, "where will you sleep?"

"Oh, I?" I answered, speaking as exuberantly as I could, "I shall do very well on the ground. But be sure to call me at the slightest sound."

Then I went out and lay down in a patch of cactus plants.

.   .   .   .   .   .

I need not dwell in detail upon the busy and arduous days that followed our landing upon the island. I had much to do. Each morning I took our latitude and longitude. By this I then set my watch, cooked porridge, and picked flowers till Miss Croyden appeared.

With every day the girl came forth from her habitation as a new surprise in her radiant beauty. One morning she had bound a cluster of wild arbutus about her brow. Another day she had twisted a band of convolvulus around her waist. On a third she had wound herself up in a mat of bulrushes.

With her bare feet and wild bulrushes all around her, she looked as a cave woman might have looked, her eyes radiant with the Caribbean dawn. My whole frame thrilled at the sight of her. At times it was all I could do not to tear the bulrushes off her and beat her with the heads of them. But I schooled myself to restraint, and handed her a rock to sit upon, and passed her her porridge on the end of a shovel with the calm politeness of a friend.

Our breakfast over, my more serious labours of the day began. I busied myself with hauling rocks or boulders along the sand to build us a house against the rainy season. With some tackle from the raft I had made myself a set of harness, by means of which I hitched myself to a boulder. By getting Miss Croyden to beat me over the back with a stick, I found that I made fair progress.

But even as I worked thus for our common comfort, my mind was fiercely filled with the thought of Edith Croyden. I knew that if once the barriers broke everything would be swept away. Heaven alone knows the effort that it cost me. At times nothing but the sternest resolution could hold my fierce impulses in check. Once I came upon the girl writing in the sand with a stick. I looked to see what she had written. I read my own name "Harold." With a wild cry I leapt into the sea and dived to the bottom of it. When I came up I was calmer. Edith came towards me ; all dripping as I was, she placed her hands upon my shoulders. " How grand you are ! " she said. " I am," I answered ; then I added, " Miss Croyden, for Heaven's sake don't touch me on the ear. I can't stand it." I turned from her and looked out over the sea. Presently I heard something like a groan behind me. The girl had thrown herself on the sand and was coiled up in a hoop. " Miss Croyden," I said, " for God's sake don't coil up in a hoop."

I rushed to the beach and rubbed gravel on my face.

With such activities, alternated with wild bursts of restraint, our life on the island passed as rapidly as in a dream. Had I not taken care to notch the days upon a stick and then cover the stick with tar, I could not have known the passage of the time. The wearing out of our clothing had threatened a serious difficulty. But by good fortune I had seen a large black and white goat wandering among the rocks and had chased it to a standstill. From its skin, leaving the fur still on, Edith had fashioned us clothes. Our boots we had replaced with alligator hide. I had, by a lucky chance, found an alligator upon the beach, and attaching a string to the fellow's neck I had led him to our camp. I had then poisoned the fellow with tinned salmon and removed his hide.

Our costume was now brought into harmony with our surroundings. For myself, garbed in goatskin with the hair outside, with alligator sandals on my feet and with whiskers at least six inches long, I have no doubt that I resembled the beau ideal of a cave man. With the open-air life a new agility seemed to have come into my limbs. With a single leap in my alligator sandals I was enabled to spring into a coco-nut tree.

As for Edith Croyden, I can only say that as she stood beside me on the beach in her suit of black goatskin (she had chosen the black spots) there were times when I felt like seizing her in the frenzy of my passion and hurling her into the sea. Fur always acts on me just like that.

It was at the opening of the fifth week of our life upon the island that a new and more surprising turn was given to our adventure. It arose out of a certain curiosity, harmless enough, on Edith Croyden's part. "Mr. Borus," she said one morning, "I should like so much to see the rest of our island. Can we?"

"Alas, Miss Croyden," I said, "I fear that there is but little to see. Our island, so far as I can judge, is merely one of the uninhabited keys of the West Indies. It is nothing but rock and sand and scrub. There is no life upon it. I fear," I added, speaking as jauntily as I could, "that unless we are taken off it we are destined to stay on it."

"Still I should like to see it," she persisted.

"Come on, then," I answered, "if you are good for a climb we can take a look over the ridge of rocks where I went up on the first day."

We made our way across the sand of the beach, among the rocks and through the close matted scrub, beyond which an eminence of rugged boulders shut out the further view.

Making our way to the top of this we obtained a wide look over the sea. The island stretched away to a considerable distance to the eastward, widening as it went, the complete view of it being shut off by similar and higher ridges of rock.

But it was the nearer view, the foreground, that at once arrested our attention. Edith seized my arm. "Look, oh, look!" she said.

Down just below us on the right hand was

a similar beach to the one that we had left. A rude hut had been erected on it and various articles lay strewn about.

Seated on a rock with their backs towards us were a man and a woman. The man was dressed in goatskins, and his whiskers, so I inferred from what I could see of them from the side, were at least as exuberant as mine. The woman was in white fur with a fillet of seaweed round her head. They were sitting close together as if in earnest colloquy.

"Cave people," whispered Edith, "aborigines of the island."

But I answered nothing. Something in the tall outline of the seated woman held my eye. A cruel presentiment stabbed me to the heart.

In my agitation my foot overset a stone, which rolled noisily down the rocks. The noise attracted the attention of the two seated below us. They turned and looked searchingly towards the place where we were concealed. Their faces were in plain sight. As I looked at that of the woman I felt my heart cease beating and the colour leave my face.

I looked into Edith's face. It was as pale as mine.

"What does it mean?" she whispered.

"Miss Croyden," I answered, "Edith—it means this. I have never found the courage to tell you. I am a married man. The woman seated there is my wife. And I love you."

Edith put out her arms with a low cry and clasped me about the neck. "Harold," she murmured, "my Harold."

"Have I done wrong?" I whispered.

"Only what I have done too," she answered. "I, too, am married, Harold, and the man sitting there below, John Croyden, is my husband."

With a wild cry such as a cave man might have uttered, I had leapt to my feet.

"Your husband!" I shouted. "Then, by the living God, he or I shall never leave this place alive."

He saw me coming as I bounded down the rocks. In an instant he had sprung to his feet. He gave no cry. He asked no question. He

168

stood erect as a cave man would, waiting for
his enemy.

And there upon the sands beside the sea
we fought, barehanded and weaponless. We
fought as cave men fight.

For a while we circled round one another,
growling. We circled four times, each watching for an opportunity. Then I picked up a
great handful of sand and threw it flap into
his face. He grabbed a coco-nut and hit me
with it in the stomach. Then I seized a twisted
strand of wet seaweed and landed him with it
behind the ear. For a moment he staggered.
Before he could recover I jumped forward,
seized him by the hair, slapped his face twice
and then leaped behind a rock. Looking from
the side I could see that Croyden, though half
dazed, was feeling round for something to
throw. To my horror I saw a great stone lying
ready to his hand. Beside me was nothing.
I gave myself up for lost, when at that very
moment I heard Edith's voice behind me saying, " The shovel, quick, the shovel ! " The
noble girl had rushed back to our encampment

and had fetched me the shovel. "Swat him with that," she cried. I seized the shovel, and with the roar of a wounded bull—or as near as I could make it—I rushed out from the rock, the shovel swung over my head.

But the fight was all out of Croyden.

"Don't strike," he said, "I'm all in. I couldn't stand a crack with that kind of thing."

He sat down upon the sand, limp. Seen thus, he somehow seemed to be quite a small man, not a cave man at all. His goatskin suit shrunk in on him. I could hear his pants as he sat.

"I surrender," he said. "Take both the women. They are yours."

I stood over him leaning upon the shovel. The two women had closed in near to us.

"I suppose you are *her* husband, are you?" Croyden went on.

I nodded.

"I thought you were. Take her."

Meantime Clara had drawn nearer to me. She looked somehow very beautiful with her golden hair in the sunlight, and the white furs draped about her.

"Harold!" she exclaimed. "Harold, is it you? How strange and masterful you look. I didn't know you were so strong."

I turned sternly towards her.

"When I was alone," I said, "on the Himalayas hunting the humpo or humped buffalo——"

Clara clasped her hands, looking into my face.

"Yes," she said, "tell me about it."

Meantime I could see that Edith had gone over to John Croyden.

"John," she said, "you shouldn't sit on the wet sand like that. You will get a chill. Let me help you to get up."

I looked at Clara and at Croyden.

"How has this happened?" I asked. "Tell me."

"We were on the same ship," Croyden said. "There came a great storm. Even the Captain had never seen——"

"I know," I interrupted, "so had ours."

"The ship struck a rock, and blew out her four funnels——"

"Ours did too," I nodded.

"The bowsprit was broken, and the steward's pantry was carried away. The Captain gave orders to leave the ship——"

"It is enough, Croyden," I said, "I see it all now. You were left behind when the boats cleared, by what accident you don't know——"

"I don't," said Croyden.

"As best you could, you constructed a raft, and with such haste as you might you placed on it such few things——"

"Exactly," he said, "a chronometer, a sextant——"

"I know," I continued, "two quadrants, a bucket of water, and a lightning rod. I presume you picked up Clara floating in the sea."

"I did," Croyden said ; "she was unconscious when I got her, but by rubbing——"

"Croyden," I said, raising the shovel again, "cut that out."

"I'm sorry," he said.

"It's all right. But you needn't go on. I

172

see all the rest of your adventures plainly enough."

"Well, I'm done with it all anyway," said Croyden gloomily. "You can do what you like. As for me, I've got a decent suit back there at our camp, and I've got it dried and pressed and I'm going to put it on."

He rose wearily, Edith standing beside him.

"What's more, Borus," he said, "I'll tell you something. This island is not uninhabited at all."

"Not uninhabited!" exclaimed Clara and Edith together. I saw each of them give a rapid look at her goatskin suit.

"Nonsense, Croyden," I said, "this island is one of the West Indian keys. On such a key as this the pirates used to land. Here they careened their ships——"

"Did what to them?" asked Croyden.

"Careened them all over from one end to the other," I said. "Here they got water and buried treasure ; but beyond that the island was, and remained, only the home of the wild gull and the sea-mews——"

"All right," said Croyden, "only it doesn't happen to be that kind of key. It's a West Indian island all right, but there's a summer hotel on the other end of it not two miles away."

"A summer hotel!" we exclaimed.

"Yes, a hotel. I suspected it all along. I picked up a tennis racket on the beach the first day; and after that I walked over the ridge and through the jungle and I could see the roof of the hotel. Only," he added rather shamefacedly, "I didn't like to tell her."

"Oh, you coward!" cried Clara. "I could slap you."

"Don't you dare," said Edith. "I'm sure you knew it as well as he did. And anyway, I was certain of it myself. I picked up a copy of last week's paper in a lunch-basket on the beach, and hid it from Mr. Borus. I didn't want to hurt his feelings."

At that moment Croyden pointed with a cry towards the sea.

"Look," he said, "for Heaven's sake, look!"
He turned.

Less than a quarter of a mile away we could

see a large white motor launch coming round the corner. The deck was gay with awnings and bright dresses and parasols.

"Great Heavens!" said Croyden. "I know that launch. It's the Appin-Joneses'."

"The Appin-Joneses'!" cried Clara. "Why, we know them too. Don't you remember, Harold, the Sunday we spent with them on the Hudson?"

Instinctively we had all jumped for cover, behind the rocks.

"Whatever shall we do?" I exclaimed.

"We must get our things," said Edith Croyden. "Jack, if your suit is ready run and get it and stop the launch. Mrs. Borus and Mr. Borus and I can get our things straightened up while you keep them talking. My suit is nearly ready anyway; I thought some one might come. Mr. Borus, would you mind running and fetching me my things, they're all in a parcel together? And perhaps if you have a looking-glass and some pins, Mrs. Borus, I could come over and dress with you."

.   .   .   .

That same evening we found ourselves all comfortably gathered on the piazza of the Hotel Christopher Columbus. Appin-Jones insisted on making himself our host, and the story of our adventures was related again and again to an admiring audience, with the accompaniment of cigars and iced champagne. Only one detail was suppressed, by common instinct. Both Clara and I felt that it would only raise needless comment to explain that Mr. and Mrs. Croyden had occupied separate encampments.

Nor is it necessary to relate our safe and easy return to New York.

Both Clara and I found Mr. and Mrs. Croyden delightful travelling companions, though perhaps we were not sorry when the moment came to say good-bye.

" The word ' good-bye,' " I remarked to Clara, as we drove away, " is always a painful one. Oddly enough when I was hunting the humpo, or humped buffalo, of the Himalayas——"

" Do tell me about it, darling," whispered Clara, as she nestled beside me in the cab.

VI

THE KIDNAPPED
PLUMBER

A TALE OF THE NEW TIME

(Being one chapter—and quite enough—from the Reminiscences of an Operating Plumber)

M

"**P**ERSONALLY," said Thornton, speaking for the first time, "I never care to take a case that involves cellar work."

We were sitting—a little group of us—round about the fire in a comfortable corner of the Steam and Air Club. Our talk had turned, as always happens with a group of professional men, into more or less technical channels. I will not say that we were talking shop; the word has an offensive sound and might be misunderstood. But we were talking as only a group of practising plumbers—including some of the biggest men in the profession—would talk. With the exception of Everett, who had a national reputation as a Consulting Barber, and Thomas, who was a vacuum cleaner ex-

179

pert, I think we all belonged to the same profession. We had been holding a convention, and Fortescue, who had one of the biggest furnace practices in the country, had read us a paper that afternoon—a most revolutionary thing—on External Diagnosis of Defective Feed Pipes, and naturally the thing had bred discussion. Fortescue, who is one of the most brilliant men in the profession, had stoutly maintained his thesis that the only method of diagnosis for trouble in a furnace is to sit down in front of it and look at it for three days; others held out for unscrewing it and carrying it home for consideration; others of us, again, claimed that by tapping the affected spot with a wrench the pipe might be fractured in such a way as to prove that it was breakable. It was at this point that Thornton interrupted with his remark about never being willing to accept a cellar case.

Naturally all the men turned to look at the speaker. Henry Thornton, at the time of which I relate, was at the height of his reputation. Beginning, quite literally, at the bottom of the ladder, he had in twenty years of practice as an operating plumber raised himself to the top of his profession. There was much in his appearance to suggest the underlying reasons of his success. His face, as is usual with men of our calling, had something of the dreamer in it, but the bold set of the jaw indicated determination of an uncommon kind. Three times President of the Plumbers' Association, Henry Thornton had enjoyed the highest honours of his chosen profession. His book on *Nut Coal* was recognized as the last word on the subject, and had been crowned by the French Academy of Nuts.

I suppose that one of the principal reasons for his success was his singular coolness and resource. I have seen Thornton enter a kitchen, with that quiet reassuring step of his, and lay out his instruments on the table, while a kitchen tap with a broken washer was sprizzling within a few feet of him, as calmly and as quietly as if he were in his lecture-room of the Plumbers' College.

"You never go into a cellar?" asked Fortescue. "But hang it, man, I don't see how one can avoid it!"

"Well, I do avoid it," answered Thornton, "at least as far as I possibly can. I send down my solderist, of course, but personally, unless it is absolutely necessary, I never go down."

"That's all very well, my dear fellow," Fortescue cut in, "but you know as well as I do that you get case after case where the cellar diagnosis is simply vital. I had a case last week, a most interesting thing—" he turned to the group of us as he spoke—"a double lesion of a gas-pipe under a cement floor—half a dozen of my colleagues had been absolutely baffled. They had made an entirely false diagnosis, operated on the dining-room floor, which they removed and carried home, and when I was called in they had just obtained permission from the Stone Mason's Protective Association to knock down one side of the house."

"Excuse me interrupting just a minute," interjected a member of the group who hailed from a distant city, "have you much trouble about that ? I mean about knocking the sides out of houses ? ”

“ No trouble now,” said Fortescue. “ We did have. But the public is getting educated up to it. Our law now allows us to knock the side out of a house when we feel that we would really like to see what is in it. We are not allowed, of course, to build it up again.”

“ No, of course not,” said the other speaker. “ But I suppose you can throw the bricks out on the lawn.”

“ Yes,” said Fortescue, “ and sit on them to eat lunch. We had a big fight in the legislature over that, but we got it through.”

“ Thank you, but I feel I am interrupting.”

“ Well, I was only saying that, as soon as I had made up my mind that the trouble was in the cellar, the whole case was simple. I took my colleagues down at once, and we sat on the floor of the cellar and held a consultation till the overpowering smell of gas convinced me that there was nothing for it but an operation on the floor. The whole thing was most successful. I was very glad, as it happened that the proprietor of the house was a very decent fellow, employed, I think, as a manager of a bank, or something of the sort. He was most grateful. It was he who gave me the engraved monkey wrench that some of you were admiring before dinner. After we had finished the whole operation—I forgot to say that we had thrown the coal out on the lawn to avoid any complication—he quite broke down. He offered us to take his whole house and keep it."

"You don't do that, do you?" asked the outsider.

"Oh no, never," said Fortescue. "We've made a very strict professional rule against it. We found that some of the younger men were apt to take a house when they were given it, and we had to frown down on it. But, gentlemen, I feel that when Mr. Thornton says that he never goes down into a cellar there must be a story behind it. I think we should invite him to relate it to us."

A murmur of assent greeted the speaker's suggestion. For myself I was particularly pleased, inasmuch as I have long felt that

184

Thornton as a *raconteur* was almost as interesting as in the rôle of an operating plumber. I have often told him that, if he had not happened to meet success in his chosen profession, he could have earned a living as a day writer : a suggestion which he has always taken in good part and without offence.

Those of my readers who have looked through the little volume of Reminiscences which I have put together, will recall the narrative of *The Missing Nut* and the little tale entitled *The Blue Blow Torch* as instances in point.

"Not much of a story, perhaps," said Thornton, "but such as it is you are welcome to it. So, if you will just fill up your glasses with raspberry vinegar, you may have the tale for what it is worth."

We gladly complied with the suggestion and Thornton continued :

"It happened a good many years ago at a time when I was only a young fellow fresh from college, very proud of my Plumb. B., and inclined to think that I knew it all. I had done a little monograph on *Choked Feed in the Blow Torch*, which had attracted attention, and I suppose that altogether I was about as conceited a young puppy as one would find in the profession. I should mention that at this time I was not married, but had set up a modest apartment of my own with a consulting-room and a single manservant. Naturally I could not afford the services of a solderist or a gassist and did everything for myself, though Simmons, my man, could at a pinch be utilized to tear down plaster and break furniture."

Thornton paused to take a sip of raspberry vinegar and went on :

"Well, then. I had come home to dinner particularly tired after a long day. I had sat in an attic the greater part of the afternoon (a case of top story valvular trouble) and had had to sit in a cramped position which practically forbade sleep. I was feeling, therefore, none too well pleased, when a little while after dinner the bell rang and Simmons brought word to the library that there was a client in the consulting-room. I reminded the fellow that I could not possibly consider a case at such an advanced hour unless I were paid emergency overtime wages with time and a half during the day of recovery."

"One moment," interrupted the outside member. "You don't mention compensation for mental shock. Do you not draw that here?"

"We do *now*," explained Thornton, "but the time of which I speak is some years ago and we still got nothing for mental shock, nor disturbance of equilibrium. Nowadays, of course, one would insist on a substantial retainer in advance.

"Well, to continue. Simmons, to my surprise, told me that he had already informed the client of this fact, and that the answer had only been a plea that the case was too urgent to admit of delay. He also supplied the further information that the client was a young lady. I am afraid," added Thornton, looking round his audience with a sympathetic smile, "that Simmons (I had got him from Harvard and he had not yet quite learned his place) even said something about her being strikingly handsome."

A general laugh greeted Thornton's announcement.

"After all," said Fortescue, "I never could see why an Ice Man should be supposed to have a monopoly on gallantry."

"Oh, I don't know," said Thornton. "For my part—I say it without affectation—the moment I am called in professionally, women, as women, cease to exist for me. I can stand beside them in the kitchen and explain to them the feed tap of a kitchen range without feeling them to be anything other than simply clients. And for the most part, I think, they reciprocate that attention. There are women, of course, who will call a man in with motives—but that's another story. I must get back to what I was saying.

"On entering the consulting-room I saw at once that Simmons had exaggerated nothing in describing my young client as beautiful. I have seldom, even among our own class, seen a more strikingly handsome girl. She was

dressed in a very plain and simple fashion
which showed me at once that she belonged
merely to the capitalist class. I am, as I think
you know, something of an observer, and my
eye at once noted the absence of heavy gold
ear-rings and wrist-bangles. The blue feathers
at the side of her hat were none of them more
than six inches long, and the buttons on her
jacket were so inconspicuous that one would
hardly notice them. In short, while her dress
was no doubt good and serviceable, there was
an absence of *chic*, a lack of noise about it, that
told at once the tale of narrow circumstances.

" She was evidently in great distress.

" ' Oh, Mr. Thornton,' she exclaimed, advancing towards me, 'do come to our house
at once. I simply don't know what to do.'

" She spoke with great emotion, and seemed
almost on the point of breaking into tears.

" ' Pray, calm yourself, my dear young
lady,' I said, 'and try to tell me what is the
trouble.'

" ' Oh, don't lose any time,' she said, 'do, do
come at once.'

" 'We will lose no time I said reassuringly, as I looked at my watch. 'It is now seven-thirty. We will reckon the time from now, with overtime at time and a half. But if I am to do anything for you I must have some idea of what has happened.'

" 'The cellar boiler,' she moaned, clasping her hands together, 'the cellar boiler won't work!'

" 'Ah!' I said soothingly. 'The cellar boiler won't work. Now tell me, is the feed choked, miss?'

" 'I don't know,' she exclaimed.

" 'Have you tried letting off the exhaust?'

" She shook her head with a doleful look.

" 'I don't know what it is,' she said.

" But already I was hastily gathering together a few instruments, questioning her rapidly as I did so.

" 'How's your pressure gauge?' I asked. 'How's your water? Do you draw from the mains or are you on the high level reservoir?'

" It had occurred to me at once that it might

be merely a case of stoppage of her main feed, complicated, perhaps, with a valvular trouble in her exhaust. On the other hand it was clear enough that, if her feed was full and her gauges working, her trouble was more likely a leak somewhere in her piping.

"But all attempts to draw from the girl any clear idea of the symptoms were unavailing. All she could tell me was that the cellar boiler wouldn't work. Beyond that her answers were mere confusion. I gathered enough, however, to feel sure that her main feed was still working, and that her top story check valve was probably in order. With that I had to be content.

"As a young practitioner, I had as yet no motor car. Simmons, however, summoned me a taxi, into which I hurriedly placed the girl and my basket of instruments, and was soon speeding in the direction she indicated. It was a dark, lowering night, with flecks of rain against the windows of the cab, and there was something in the lateness of the hour (it was now after half-past eight) and the nature of my mission which gave me a stimulating sense

of adventure. The girl directed me, as I felt
sure she would, towards the capitalist quarter
of the town. We had soon sped away from
the brightly lighted streets and tall apartment
buildings among which my usual practice lay,
and entered the gloomy and dilapidated section
of the city where the unhappy capitalist class
reside. I need not remind those of you who
know it that it is scarcely a cheerful place to
find oneself in after nightfall. The thick
growth of trees, the silent gloom of the ill-
lighted houses, and the rank undergrowth of
shrubs give it an air of desolation, not to say
danger. It is certainly not the place that a
professional man would choose to be abroad in
after dark. The inhabitants, living, so it is
said, on their scanty dividends and on such
parts of their income as our taxation is still
unable to reach, are not people that one would
care to fall in with after nightfall.

"Since the time of which I speak we have
done much to introduce a better state of things.
The opening of day schools of carpentry,
plumbing and calcimining for the children of

the capitalist is already producing results. Strange though it may seem, one of the most brilliant of our boiler fitters of to-day was brought up haphazard in this very quarter of the town and educated only by a French governess and a university tutor. But at the time practically nothing had been done. The place was infested with consumers, and there were still, so it was said, servants living in some of the older houses. A butler had been caught one night in a thick shrubbery beside one of the gloomy streets.

"We alighted at one of the most sombre of the houses, and our taxi-driver, with evident relief, made off in the darkness.

"The girl admitted us into a dark hall, where she turned on an electric light. 'We have light,' she said, with that peculiar touch of pride that one sees so often in her class, 'we have four bulbs.'

"Then she called down a flight of stairs that apparently led to the cellar :

"'Father, the plumber has come. Do come up now, dear, and rest.'

"A step sounded on the stairs, and there appeared beside us one of the most forbidding-looking men that I have ever beheld. I don't know whether any of you have ever seen an Anglican Bishop. Probably not. Outside of the bush, they are now never seen. But at the time of which I speak there were a few still here and there in the purlieus of the city. The man before us was tall and ferocious, and his native ferocity was further enhanced by the heavy black beard which he wore in open defiance of the compulsory shaving laws. His black shovel-shaped hat and his black clothes lent him a singularly sinister appearance, while his legs were bound in tight gaiters, as if ready for an instant spring. He carried in his hand an enormous monkey wrench, on which his fingers were clasped in a restless grip.

"'Can you fix the accursed thing?' he asked.

"I was not accustomed to being spoken to in this way, but I was willing for the girl's sake to strain professional courtesy to the limit.

"'I don't know,' I answered, 'but if you will have the goodness first to fetch me a little

194

light supper, I shall be glad to see what I can do afterwards.'

"My firm manner had its effect. With obvious reluctance the fellow served me some biscuits and some not bad champagne in the dining-room.

"The girl had meantime disappeared upstairs.

"'If you're ready now,' said the Bishop, 'come on down.'

"We went down to the cellar. It was a huge, gloomy place, with a cement floor, lighted by a dim electric bulb. I could see in the corner the outline of a large furnace (in those days the poorer classes had still no central heat) and near it a tall boiler. In front of this a man was kneeling, evidently trying to unscrew a nut, but twisting it the wrong way. He was an elderly man with a grey moustache, and was dressed, in open defiance of the law, in a military costume or uniform.

"He turned round towards us and rose from his knees.

"'I'm dashed if I can make the rotten thing go round,' he said.

" ' It's all right, General,' said the Bishop. ' I have brought a plumber.'

" For the next few minutes my professional interest absorbed all my faculties. I laid out my instruments upon a board, tapped the boiler with a small hammer, tested the feed-tube, and in a few moments had made what I was convinced was a correct diagnosis of the trouble.

But here I encountered the greatest professional dilemma in which I have ever been placed. There was nothing wrong with the boiler at all. It connected, as I ascertained at once by a thermo-dynamic valvular test, with the furnace (in fact, I could see it did), and the furnace quite evidently had been allowed to go out.

" What was I to do ? If I told them this, I broke every professional rule of our union. If the thing became known I should probably be disbarred and lose my overalls for it. It was my plain professional duty to take a large hammer and knock holes in the boiler with it, smash up the furnace pipes, start a leak of gas, and then call in three or more of my colleagues.

"But somehow I couldn't find it in my heart to do it. The thought of the girl's appealing face arose before me.

"'How long has this trouble been going on?' I asked sternly.

"'Quite a time,' answered the Bishop. 'It began, did it not, General, the same day that the confounded furnace went out? The General here and Admiral Hay and I have been working at it for three days.'

"'Well, gentlemen,' I said, 'I don't want to read you a lesson on your own ineptitude, and I don't suppose you would understand it if I did. But don't you see that the whole trouble is *because* you let the furnace out? The boiler itself is all right, but you see, gents, it feeds off the furnace.'

"'Ah,' said the Bishop in a deep melodious tone, 'it feeds off the furnace. Now that is most interesting. Let me repeat that; I must try to remember it; it feeds *off* the furnace. Just so.'

197

" The upshot was that in twenty minutes we had the whole thing put to rights. I set the General breaking up boxes and had the Bishop rake out the clinkers, and very soon we had the furnace going and the boiler in operation.

"'But now tell me,' said the Bishop, 'suppose one wanted to let the furnace out— suppose, I mean to say, that it was summer-time, and suppose one rather felt that one didn't care about a furnace and yet one wanted one's boiler going for one's hot water, and that sort of thing, what would one do?'

"'In that case,' I said, 'you couldn't run your heating off your furnace : you'd have to connect in your tubing with a gas generator.'

"'Ah, there you get me rather beyond my depth,' said the Bishop.

"The General shook his head. 'Bishop,' he said, 'just step upstairs a minute; I have an idea.'

"They went up together, leaving me below. To my surprise and consternation, as they reached the top of the cellar stairs, I saw the General swing the door shut and heard a key

198

turn in the lock. I rushed to the top of the stairs and tried in vain to open the door. I was trapped. In a moment I realized my folly in trusting myself in the hands of these people.

"I could hear their voices in the hall, apparently in eager discussion.

"'But the fellow is priceless,' the General was saying. 'We could take him round to all the different houses and make him fix them all. Hang it, Bishop, I haven't had a decent tap running for two years, and Admiral Hay's pantry has been flooded since last March.'

"'But one couldn't compel him?'

"'Certainly, why not? I'd compel him bally quick with this.'

"I couldn't see what the General referred to, but had no doubt that it was the huge wrench that he still carried in his hand.

"'We could gag the fellow,' he went on, 'take him from house to house and make him put everything right.'

"'Ah, but afterwards?' said the Bishop.

"'Afterwards,' answered the General, 'why kill him! Knock him on the head and bury him under the cement in the cellar. Hay and I could easily bury him, or for that matter I imagine one could easily use the furnace itself to dispose of him.'

" I must confess that my blood ran cold as I listened.

" 'But do you think it right ? ' objected the Bishop. 'You will say, of course, that it is only killing a plumber ; but yet one asks oneself whether it wouldn't be just a *leetle* bit unjustifiable.'

" 'Nonsense,' said the General. 'You remember that last year, when Hay strangled the income tax collector, you yourself were very keen on it.'

" 'Ah, that was different,' said the Bishop, ' one felt there that there was an end to serve, but here——'

" 'Nonsense,' repeated the General, 'come along and get Hay. He'll make short work of him.'

" I heard their retreating footsteps and then all was still.

" The horror which filled my mind as I sat

in the half darkness waiting for their return I cannot describe. My fate appeared sealed and I gave myself up for lost, when presently I heard a light step in the hall and the key turned in the lock.

" The girl stood in front of me. She was trembling with emotion.

" ' Quick, quick, Mr. Thornton,' she said. ' I heard all that they said. Oh, I think it's dreadful of them, simply dreadful. Mr. Thornton, I'm really ashamed that Father should act that way.'

" I came out into the hall still half dazed.

" ' They've gone over to Admiral Hay's house, there among the trees. That's their lantern. Please, please, don't lose a minute. Do you mind not having a cab? I think really you'd prefer not to wait. And look, won't you please take this ? '—she handed me a little packet as she spoke—' this is a piece of pie : you always get that, don't you ? and there's a bit of cheese with it, but please run.'

" In another moment I had bounded from the door into the darkness. A wild rush through the darkened streets, and in twenty minutes I was safe back again in my own consulting-room."

Thornton paused in his narrative, and at that moment one of the stewards of the club came and whispered something in his ear.

He rose.

" I'm sorry," he said, with a grave face. " I'm called away ; a very old client of mine. Valvular trouble of the worst kind. I doubt if I can do anything, but I must at least go. Please don't let me break up your evening, however."

With a courtly bow he left us.

" And do you know the sequel to Thornton's story ? " asked Fortescue with a smile.

We looked expectantly at him.

" Why, he married the girl," explained Fortescue. " You see, he had to go back to her house for his wrench. One always does."

" Of course," we exclaimed.

" In fact he went three times ; and the last time he asked the girl to marry him and she said 'yes.' He took her out of her surroundings had her educated at a cooking school, and had her given lessons on the parlour organ. She's Mrs. Thornton now."

"And the Bishop?" asked some one.

"Oh, Thornton looked after him. He got him a position heating furnaces in the synagogues. He worked at it till he died a few years ago. They say that once he got the trick of it he took the greatest delight in it. Well, I must go too. Good night."

VII

THE BLUE AND THE GREY
A PRE-WAR WAR STORY

(The title is selected for its originality. A set of seventy-five maps will be supplied to any reader free for seventy-five cents. This offer is only open till it is closed)

VII.—The Blue and the Grey: A Pre-War War Story.

CHAPTER I

THE scene was a striking one. It was night. Never had the Mississippi presented a more remarkable appearance. Broad bayous, swollen beyond our powers of description, swirled to and fro in the darkness under trees garlanded with Spanish moss. All moss other than Spanish had been swept away by the angry flood of the river.

Eggleston Lee Carey Randolph, a young Virginian, captain of the ——th company of the ——th regiment of ——'s brigade—even this is more than we ought to say, and is hard to pronounce—attached to the Army of the Tennessee, struggled in vain with the swollen

waters. At times he sank. At other times he
went up.

In the intervals he wondered whether it
would ever be possible for him to rejoin the
particular platoon of the particular regiment
to which he belonged, and of which's whereabouts (not having the volume of the army
record at hand) he was in ignorance. In the
intervals, also, he reflected on his past life to a
sufficient extent to give the reader a more or
less workable idea as to who and to what he
was. His father, the old grey-haired Virginian
aristocrat, he could see him still. "Take this
sword, Eggleston," he had said, "use it for
the State ; never for anything else : don't cut
string with it or open tin cans. Never sheathe
it till the soil of Virginia is free. Keep it
bright, my boy : oil it every now and then,
and you'll find it an A 1 sword."

Did Eggleston think, too, in his dire peril of
another—younger than his father and fairer ?
Necessarily, he did. "Go, Eggleston ! " she
had exclaimed, as they said farewell under the
portico of his father's house where she was

his prancing black charger (during this distressed period all the horses in both armies were charged : there was no other way to pay for them), and in a few terse words, about three pages, gave his views on the Constitution of the United States.

Jefferson Davis, standing up in his stirrups, delivered a stirring harangue, about six columns, on the powers of the Supreme Court, admirably calculated to rouse the soldiers to frenzy. After which General A. P. Hill offered a short address, soldier-like and to the point, on the fundamental principles of international law, which inflamed the army to the highest pitch.

At this moment an officer approached the President, saluted and stood rigidly at attention. Davis, with that nice punctilio which marked the Southern army, returned the salute.

" Do you speak first ? " he said, " or did I ? "

" Let me," said the officer. " Your Excellency," he continued, " a young Virginian officer has just been fished out of the Mississippi."

Davis's eye flashed. " Good ! " he said. " Look and see if there are many more," and then he added with a touch of melancholy, "The South needs them : fish them all out. Bring this one here."

Eggleston Lee Carey Randolph, still dripping from the waters of the bayou, was led by the faithful negroes who had rescued him before the generals. Davis, who kept every thread of the vast panorama of the war in his intricate brain, eyed him keenly and directed a few searching questions to him, such as : "Who are you ? Where are you ? What day of the week is it ? How much is nine times twelve ?" and so forth. Satisfied with Eggleston's answers, Davis sat in thought a moment, and then continued :

"I am anxious to send some one through the entire line of the Confederate armies in such a way that he will be present at all the great battles and end up at the battle of Gettysburg. Can you do it ?"

Randolph looked at his chief with a flush of pride.

"I can."

"Good !" resumed Davis. "To accomplish

this task you must carry despatches. What
they will be about I have not yet decided. But
it is customary in such cases to write them so
that they are calculated, if lost, to endanger
the entire Confederate cause. The main thing
is, can you carry them ? "

"Sir," said Eggleston, raising his hand in a
military salute, "I am a Randolph."

Davis with soldierly dignity removed his hat.
"I am proud to hear it, Captain Randolph," he
said.

"And a Carey," continued our hero.

Davis, with a graciousness all his own, took
off his gloves. "I trust you, *Major* Randolph,"
he said.

"And I am a Lee," added Eggleston quickly.

Davis with a courtly bow unbuttoned his
jacket. "It is enough," he said. "I trust you.
You shall carry the despatches. You are to
carry them on your person and, as of course
you understand, you are to keep on losing them.
You are to drop them into rivers, hide them in
old trees, bury them under moss, talk about
them in your sleep. In fact, sir," said Davis,

with a slight gesture of impatience—it was his *one* fault—"you must act towards them as any bearer of Confederate despatches is expected to act. The point is, can you do it, or can't you ? "

" Sir," said Randolph, saluting again with simple dignity, " I come from Virginia."

" Pardon me," said the President, saluting with both hands, " I had forgotten it."

CHAPTER III

RANDOLPH set out that night, mounted upon the fastest horse, in fact the fleetest, that the Confederate Army could supply. He was attended only by a dozen faithful negroes, all devoted to his person.

Riding over the Tennessee mountains by paths known absolutely to no one and never advertised, he crossed the Tombigbee, the Tahoochie and the Tallahassee, all frightfully swollen, and arrived at the headquarters of General Braxton Bragg.

At this moment Bragg was extended over some seven miles of bush and dense swamp. His front rested on the marshes of the Tahoochie River, while his rear was doubled sharply back and rested on a dense growth of cactus plants. Our readers can thus form a fairly accurate idea of Bragg's position. Over against him, not more than fifty miles to the north, his indomitable opponent, Grant, lay in a frog-swamp. The space between them was filled with Union and Confederate pickets, fraternizing, joking, roasting corn, and firing an occasional shot at one another.

One glance at Randolph's despatches was enough.

"Take them at once to General Hood," said Bragg.

"Where is he?" asked Eggleston, with military precision.

Bragg waved his sword towards the east. It was characteristic of the man that even on active service he carried a short sword, while a pistol, probably loaded, protruded from his belt. But such was Bragg. Anyway, he waved his sword. "Over there beyond the Tahoochi-caba range," he said. "Do you know it ?"

"No," said Randolph, "but I can find it."

"Do," said Bragg, and added, "One thing more. On your present mission let nothing stop you. Go forward at all costs. If you come to a river, swim it. If you come to a tree, cut it down. If you strike a fence, climb over it. But don't stop ! If you are killed, never mind. Do you understand ?"

"Almost," said Eggleston.

Two days later Eggleston reached the head-quarters of General Hood, and flung himself, rather than dismounted, from his jaded horse.

"Take me to the General !" he gasped.

They pointed to the log cabin in which General Hood was quartered.

Eggleston flung himself, rather than stepped, through the door.

Hood looked up from the table.

"Who was that flung himself in ?" he asked.

Randolph reached out his hand. "Despatches !" he gasped. "Food, whisky !"

" Poor lad," said the General, "you are exhausted. When did you last have food ? "

" Yesterday morning," gasped Eggleston.

" You're lucky," said Hood bitterly. "And when did you last have a drink ? "

" Two weeks ago," answered Randolph.

" Great Heaven ! " said Hood, starting up. " Is it possible ? Here, quick, drink it ! "

He reached out a bottle of whisky. Randolph drained it to the last drop.

" Now, General," he said, " I am at your service."

Meanwhile Hood had cast his eye over the despatches.

" Major Randolph," he said, " you have seen General Bragg ? "

" I have."

" And Generals Johnston and Smith ? "

" Yes."

" You have been through Mississippi and Tennessee and seen all the battles there ? "

" I have," said Randolph.

" Then," said Hood, " there is nothing left except to send you at once to the army in

Virginia under General Lee. Remount your horse at once and ride to Gettysburg. Lose no time."

CHAPTER IV

IT was at Gettysburg in Pennsylvania that Randolph found General Lee.

The famous field is too well known to need description. The armies of the North and the South lay in and around the peaceful village of Gettysburg. About it the yellow cornfields basked in the summer sun. The voices of the teachers and the laughter of merry children rose in the harvest-fields. But already the shadow of war was falling over the landscape. As soon as the armies arrived, the shrewder of the farmers suspected that there would be trouble.

General Lee was seated gravely on his horse, looking gravely over the ground before him.

"Major Randolph," said the Confederate

chieftain gravely, "you are just in time. We are about to go into action. I need your advice."

Randolph bowed. "Ask me anything you like," he said.

"Do you like the way I have the army placed?" asked Lee.

Our hero directed a searching look over the field. "Frankly, I don't," he said.

"What's the matter with it?" questioned Lee eagerly. "I felt there was something wrong myself. What is it?"

"Your left," said Randolph, "is too far advanced. It sticks out."

"By Heaven!" said Lee, turning to General Longstreet, "the boy is right! Is there anything else?"

"Yes," said Randolph, "your right is crooked. It is all sideways."

"It is. It is!" said Lee, striking his forehead. "I never noticed it. I'll have it straightened at once. Major Randolph, if the Confederate cause is saved, you, and you alone, have saved it."

"One thing more," said Randolph. "Is your artillery loaded?"

"Major Randolph," said Lee, speaking very gravely, "you have saved us again. I never thought of it."

At this moment a bullet sang past Eggleston's ear. He smiled.

"The battle has begun," he murmured. Another bullet buzzed past his other ear. He laughed softly to himself. A shell burst close to his feet. He broke into uncontrolled laughter. This kind of thing always amused him. Then, turning grave in a moment, "Put General Lee under cover," he said to those about him, "spread something over him."

In a few moments the battle was raging in all directions. The Confederate Army was nominally controlled by General Lee, but in reality by our hero. Eggleston was everywhere. Horses were shot under him. Mules were shot around him and behind him. Shells exploded all over him; but with undaunted courage he continued to wave his sword in all directions, riding wherever the fight was hottest.

The battle raged for three days.

On the third day of the conflict, Randolph, his coat shot to rags, his hat pierced, his trousers practically useless, still stood at Lee's side, urging and encouraging him.

Mounted on his charger, he flew to and fro in all parts of the field, moving the artillery, leading the cavalry, animating and directing the infantry. In fact, he was the whole battle.

But his efforts were in vain.

He turned sadly to General Lee. "It is bootless," he said.

"What is?" asked Lee.

"The army," said Randolph. "We must withdraw it."

"Major Randolph," said the Confederate chief, "I yield to your superior knowledge. We must retreat."

A few hours later the Confederate forces, checked but not beaten, were retiring southward towards Virginia.

Eggleston, his head sunk in thought, rode in the rear.

As he thus slowly neared a farmhouse, a

woman—a girl—flew from it towards him with outstretched arms.

"Eggleston!" she cried.

Randolph flung himself from his horse. "Leonora!" he gasped. "You here! In all this danger! How comes it? What brings you here?"

"We live here," she said. "This is Pa's house. This is our farm. Gettysburg is our home. Oh, Egg, it has been dreadful, the noise of the battle! We couldn't sleep for it. Pa's all upset about it. But come in. Do come in. Dinner's nearly ready."

Eggleston gazed a moment at the retreating army. Duty and affection struggled in his heart.

"I will," he said.

CHAPTER V

CONCLUSION

The strife is done. The conflict has ceased. The wounds are healed. North and South are

222

one. East and West are even less. The Civil War is over. Lee is dead. Grant is buried in New York. The Union Pacific runs from Omaha to San Francisco. There is total prohibition in the United States. The output of dressed beef last year broke all records.

And Eggleston Lee Carey Randolph survives, hale and hearty, bright and cheery, free and easy—and so forth. There is grey hair upon his temples (some, not much), and his step has lost something of its elasticity (not a great deal), and his form is somewhat bowed (though not really crooked).

But he still lives there in the farmstead at Gettysburg, and Leonora, now, like himself, an old woman, is still at his side.

You may see him any day. In fact, he is the old man who shows you over the battlefield for fifty cents and explains how he himself fought and won the great battle.

VIII
BUGGAM GRANGE
A GOOD OLD GHOST STORY

P

VIII.—*Buggam Grange: A Good Old Ghost Story.*

THE evening was already falling as
the vehicle in which I was contained
entered upon the long and gloomy
avenue that leads to Buggam Grange.

A resounding shriek echoed through the
wood as I entered the avenue. I paid no attention to it at the moment, judging it to be
merely one of those resounding shrieks which
one might expect to hear in such a place at
such a time. As my drive continued, however
I found myself wondering in spite of myself
why such a shriek should have been uttered at
the very moment of my approach.

I am not by temperament in any degree a
nervous man, and yet there was much in my
surroundings to justify a certain feeling of

apprehension. The Grange is situated in the loneliest part of England, the marsh country of the fens to which civilization has still hardly penetrated. The inhabitants, of whom there are only one and a half to the square mile, live here and there among the fens and eke out a miserable existence by frog-fishing and catching flies. They speak a dialect so broken as to be practically unintelligible, while the perpetual rain which falls upon them renders speech itself almost superfluous.

Here and there where the ground rises slightly above the level of the fens there are dense woods tangled with parasitic creepers and filled with owls. Bats fly from wood to wood. The air on the lower ground is charged with the poisonous gases which exude from the marsh, while in the woods it is heavy with the dank odours of deadly nightshade and poison ivy.

It had been raining in the afternoon, and as I drove up the avenue the mournful dripping of the rain from the dark trees accentuated the cheerlessness of the gloom. The vehicle in which I rode was a fly on three wheels, the fourth having apparently been broken and taken off, causing the fly to sag on one side and drag on its axle over the muddy ground, the fly thus moving only at a foot's pace in a way calculated to enhance the dreariness of the occasion. The driver on the box in front of me was so thickly muffled up as to be indistinguishable, while the horse which drew us was so thickly coated with mist as to be practically invisible. Seldom, I may say, have I had a drive of so mournful a character.

The avenue presently opened out upon a lawn with overgrown shrubberies, and in the half darkness I could see the outline of the Grange itself, a rambling, dilapidated building. A dim light struggled through the casement of a window in a tower room. Save for the melancholy cry of a row of owls sitting on the roof, and croaking of the frogs in the moat which ran around the grounds, the place was soundless. My driver halted his horse at the hither side of the moat. I tried in vain to urge him, by signs, to go further. I could see by the fellow's face that he was in a paroxysm of fear, and indeed nothing but the extra sixpence which I had added to his fare would have made him undertake the drive up the avenue. I had no sooner alighted than he wheeled his cab about and made off.

Laughing heartily at the fellow's trepidation (I have a way of laughing heartily in the dark), I made my way to the door and pulled the bell-handle. I could hear the muffled reverberations of the bell far within the building. Then all was silent. I bent my ear to listen, but could hear nothing except, perhaps, the sound of a low moaning as of a person in pain or in great mental distress. Convinced, however, from what my friend Sir Jeremy Buggam had told me, that the Grange was not empty, I raised the ponderous knocker and beat with it loudly against the door.

But perhaps at this point I may do well to explain to my readers (before they are too frightened to listen to me) how I came to be beating on the door of Buggam Grange at nightfall on a gloomy November evening.

A year before I had been sitting with Sir Jeremy Buggam, the present baronet, on the verandah of his ranch in California.

"So you don't believe in the supernatural?" he was saying.

"Not in the slightest," I answered, lighting a cigar as I spoke. When I want to speak very positively, I generally light a cigar as I speak.

"Well, at any rate, Digby," said Sir Jeremy, "Buggam Grange is haunted. If you want to be assured of it go down there any time and spend the night and you'll see for yourself."

"My dear fellow," I replied, "nothing will give me greater pleasure. I shall be back in England in six weeks, and I shall be delighted to put your ideas to the test. Now tell me," I added somewhat cynically, "is there any particular season or day when your Grange is supposed to be specially terrible?"

Sir Jeremy looked at me strangely. "Why do you ask that?" he said. "Have you heard the story of the Grange?"

"Never heard of the place in my life," I answered cheerily. "Till you mentioned it to-night, my dear fellow, I hadn't the remotest idea that you still owned property in England."

"The Grange is shut up," said Sir Jeremy, "and has been for twenty years. But I keep a man there—Horrod—he was butler in my father's time and before. If you care to go, I'll write him that you're coming. And, since you are taking your own fate in your hands, the fifteenth of November is the day."

At that moment Lady Buggam and Clara and the other girls came trooping out on the verandah, and the whole thing passed clean out of my mind. Nor did I think of it again until I was back in London. Then, by one of those strange coincidences or premonitions— call it what you will—it suddenly occurred to me one morning that it was the fifteenth of November. Whether Sir Jeremy had written to Horrod or not, I did not know. But none the less nightfall found me, as I have described, knocking at the door of Buggam Grange.

The sound of the knocker had scarcely ceased to echo when I heard the shuffling of feet within, and the sound of chains and bolts being withdrawn. The door opened. A man stood before me holding a lighted candle which he shaded with his hand. His faded black clothes, once apparently a butler's dress, his white hair and advanced age left me in no doubt that he was Horrod of whom Sir Jeremy had spoken.

Without a word he motioned me to come in, and, still without speech, he helped me to remove my wet outer garments, and then beckoned me into a great room, evidently the dining-room of the Grange.

I am not in any degree a nervous man by temperament, as I think I remarked before, and yet there was something in the vastness of the wainscoted room, lighted only by a single candle, and in the silence of the empty house, and still more in the appearance of my speechless attendant, which gave me a feeling of distinct uneasiness. As Horrod moved to and fro I took occasion to scrutinize his face more narrowly. I have seldom seen features more calculated to inspire a nervous dread. The pallor of his face and the whiteness of his hair (the man was at least seventy), and still more the peculiar furtiveness of his eyes, seemed to mark him as one who lived under a great terror. He moved with a noiseless step and at times he turned his head to glance in the dark corners of the room.

"Sir Jeremy told me," I said, speaking as loudly and as heartily as I could, "that he would apprise you of my coming."

I was looking into his face as I spoke.

In answer Horrod laid his finger across his lips and I knew that he was deaf and dumb. I am not nervous (I think I said that), but the realization that my sole companion in the empty house was a deaf mute struck a cold chill to my heart.

Horrod laid in front of me a cold meat pie, a cold goose, a cheese, and a tall flagon of cider. But my appetite was gone. I ate the goose, but found that after I had finished the pie I had but little zest for the cheese, which I finished without enjoyment. The cider had a sour taste, and after having permitted

Horrod to refill the flagon twice I found that it induced a sense of melancholy and decided to drink no more.

My meal finished, the butler picked up the candle and beckoned me to follow him. We passed through the empty corridors of the house, a long line of pictured Buggams looking upon us as we passed, their portraits in the flickering light of the taper assuming a strange and life-like appearance, as if leaning forward from their frames to gaze upon the intruder.

Horrod led me upstairs and I realized that he was taking me to the tower in the east wing, in which I had observed a light.

The rooms to which the butler conducted me consisted of a sitting-room with an adjoining bedroom, both of them fitted with antique wainscoting against which a faded tapestry fluttered. There was a candle burning on the table in the sitting-room, but its insufficient light only rendered the surroundings the more dismal. Horrod bent down in front of the fireplace and endeavoured to light a fire there.

But the wood was evidently damp and the fire flickered feebly on the hearth.

The butler left me, and in the stillness of the house I could hear his shuffling step echo down the corridor. It may have been fancy, but it seemed to me that his departure was the signal for a low moan that came from somewhere behind the wainscot. There was a narrow cupboard door at one side of the room, and for the moment I wondered whether the moaning came from within. I am not as a rule lacking in courage (I am sure my reader will be decent enough to believe this), yet I found myself entirely unwilling to open the cupboard door and look within. In place of doing so I seated myself in a great chair in front of the feeble fire. I must have been seated there for some time when I happened to lift my eyes to the mantel above and saw, standing upon it, a letter addressed to myself. I knew the handwriting at once to be that of Sir Jeremy Buggam.

I opened it, and spreading it out within reach of the feeble candlelight, I read as follows :

" My dear Digby,

"In our talk that you will remember, I had no time to finish telling you about the mystery of Buggam Grange. I take for granted, however, that you will go there and that Horrod will put you in the tower rooms, which are the only ones that make any pretence of being habitable. I have, therefore, sent him this letter to deliver at the Grange itself.

"The story is this :

"On the night of the fifteenth of November, fifty years ago, my grandfather was murdered in the room in which you are sitting, by his cousin, Sir Duggam Buggam. He was stabbed from behind while seated at the little table at which you are probably reading this letter. The two had been playing cards at the table and my grandfather's body was found lying in a litter of cards and gold sovereigns on the floor. Sir Duggam Buggam, insensible from drink, lay beside him, the fatal knife at his hand, his fingers smeared with blood. My grandfather, though of the younger branch, possessed a part of the estates which were to revert to Sir Duggam on his death. Sir Duggam Buggam was tried at the Assizes and was hanged. On the day of his execution he was permitted by the authorities, out of respect for his rank, to wear a mask to the scaffold. The clothes in which he was executed are hanging at full length in the little cupboard to your right, and the mask is above them. It is said that on every fifteenth of November at midnight the cupboard door opens and Sir Duggam Buggam walks out into the room. It has been found impossible to get servants to remain at the Grange, and the place—except for the presence of Horrod—has been unoccupied for a generation. At the time of the murder Horrod was a young man of twenty-two, newly entered into the service of the family. It was he who entered the room and discovered the crime. On the day of the execution he was stricken with paralysis and has never spoken since. From that time to this he has never consented to leave the Grange, where he lives in isolation.

"Wishing you a pleasant night after your
tiring journey,

"I remain,

"Very faithfully,

"JEREMY BUGGAM."

I leave my reader to imagine my state of
mind when I completed the perusal of the
letter.

I have as little belief in the supernatural as
anyone, yet I must confess that there was something in the surroundings in which I now found
myself which rendered me at least uncomfort-
able. My reader may smile if he will, but I
assure him that it was with a very distinct feeling of uneasiness that I at length managed to
rise to my feet, and, grasping my candle in my
hand, to move backward into the bedroom. As
I backed into it something so like a moan
seemed to proceed from the closed cupboard
that I accelerated my backward movement to a
considerable degree. I hastily blew out the
candle, threw myself upon the bed and drew
the bedclothes over my head, keeping,

239

however, one eye and one ear still out and available.

How long I lay thus listening to every sound, I cannot tell. The stillness had become absolute. From time to time I could dimly hear the distant cry of an owl, and once far away in the building below a sound as of some one dragging a chain along a floor. More than once I was certain that I heard the sound of moaning behind the wainscot. Meantime I realized that the hour must now be drawing close upon the fatal moment of midnight. My watch I could not see in the darkness, but by reckoning the time that must have elapsed I knew that midnight could not be far away. Then presently my ear, alert to every sound, could just distinguish far away across the fens the striking of a church bell, in the clock tower of Buggam village church, no doubt, tolling the hour of twelve.

On the last stroke of twelve, the cupboard door in the next room opened. There is no need to ask me how I knew it. I couldn't, of course, see it, but I could hear, or sense in some way, the sound of it. I could feel my hair, all of it, rising upon my head. I was aware that there was a *presence* in the adjoining room, I will not say a person, a living soul, but a *presence*. Anyone who has been in the next room to a presence will know just how I felt. I could hear a sound as of some one groping on the floor and the faint rattle as of coins.

My hair was now perpendicular. My reader can blame it or not, but it was.

Then at this very moment from somewhere below in the building there came the sound of a prolonged and piercing cry, a cry as of a soul passing in agony. My reader may censure me or not, but right at this moment I decided to beat it. Whether I should have remained to see what was happening is a question that I will not discuss. My one idea was to get out, and to get out quickly. The window of the tower room was some twenty-five feet above the ground. I sprang out through the casement in one leap and landed on the grass below. I jumped over the shrubbery in one bound and cleared the moat in one jump. I went down the avenue in about six strides and ran five miles along the road through the fens in three minutes. This at least is an accurate transcription of my sensations. It may have taken longer. I never stopped till I found myself on the threshold of the *Buggam Arms* in Little Buggam, beating on the door for the landlord.

I returned to Buggam Grange on the next day in the bright sunlight of a frosty November morning, in a seven-cylinder motor car with six local constables and a physician. It makes all the difference. We carried revolvers, spades, pickaxes, shotguns and an ouija board.

What we found cleared up for ever the mystery of the Grange. We discovered Horrod the butler lying on the dining-room floor quite dead. The physician said that he had died from heart failure. There was evidence from the marks of his shoes in the dust that he had come in the night to the tower room. On the table he had placed a paper which contained a full confession of his having murdered Jeremy Buggam fifty years before. The circumstances of the murder had rendered it easy for him to fasten the crime upon Sir Duggam, already insensible from drink. A few minutes with the ouija board enabled us to get a full corroboration from Sir Duggam. He promised, moreover, now that his name was cleared, to go away from the premises for ever.

My friend, the present Sir Jeremy, has rehabilitated Buggam Grange. The place is rebuilt. The moat is drained. The whole house is lit with electricity. There are beautiful motor drives in all directions in the woods. He has had the bats shot and the owls stuffed. His daughter, Clara Buggam, became my wife. She is looking over my shoulder as I write. What more do you want?

THE END

THE UNSOLVED RIDDLE OF SOCIAL JUSTICE

Crown 8vo.   *5s. net*

A discussion of the new social unrest, the transformation of society which it portends and the social catastrophe which it might precipitate.

The point of view taken by the author leads towards the conclusion that the safety of the future lies in a progressive movement of social control alleviating at least the misery it cannot obliterate, and based upon the broad general principle of equality of opportunity, and a fair start. The chief immediate opportunities for social betterment, as the writer sees them, lie in the attempt to give every human being in childhood, education and opportunity.

"His book is short, lucid, always to the point, and sometimes witty."—*Times.*

"A book for the times, suggestive, critical and highly stimulating. Mr. Leacock surveys the troubled hour and discusses the popular palliatives with a keen, unbiassed intelligence and splendid sympathy. I hope it will have as large a circulation as any of his humorous books, for it has much wisdom in it."—*Daily Chronicle.*

"The charm of Mr. Leacock's book is . . . that it deals tersely and clearly with the problem of Social Justice without technical jargon or any abuse of generalities."—*Morning Post.*

LONDON : JOHN LANE, THE BODLEY HEAD

THE HUMOROUS NOVELS OF HARRY LEON WILSON

BUNKER BEAN
MA PETTENGILL
SOMEWHERE IN RED GAP
RUGGLES OF RED GAP

Crown 8vo.   7s. net.

Harry Leon Wilson is one of the first of American humorists, and in popularity he is a close rival of O. Henry. His "Ruggles of Red Gap," published at the beginning of the war, achieved a distinct success in England, while the raciness and vivacity of "Ma Pettengill" have furthered the author's reputation as an inimitable delineator of Western comedy. An English edition of this author's works is in course of preparation, of which the above are the first volumes.

"The author has the rare and precious gift of original humour."—*Daily Graphic.*

"Thackeray would have enjoyed Mr. Wilson's merry tale of 'Ruggles of Red Gap.' A very triumph of farce."—*Sunday Times.*

"Mr. Wilson is an American humorist of the first water. We have not for a long time seen anything so clever in its way and so outrageously funny."—*Literary World.*

LONDON : JOHN LANE, THE BODLEY HEAD